THE ODYSSEY

AN ADVENTURE FOR THE AGES

(BASED ON THE EPIC POEM BY HOMER)

FROM THE GREEK MYTHOLOGY SERIES

BY

G.W. BRUNSWICK

GW@TheGreekMyths.net
www.thegreekmyths.net

Library of Congress Control Number: 2023918479

The Odyssey / G.W. Brunswick -- 1st ed.
ISBN 978-1-7372999-8-1
ISBN 978-1-7372999-9-8 (eBook)

To my wife for all her support, my daughter who loves Greek mythology as much as I do, and our son-in-law who protects and defends our country.

Acknowledgements

I would like to acknowledge two people without whose support this book would not be possible, my wife Dantzler and daughter Catherine. Thank you for believing in me. Without your support this book would never have become a reality. I would also like to thank my parents for giving me the drive to set my mind to something and see it through to the end. While they are no longer with me, their influence has had a lasting effect on me.

Forward

The following is an adaptation of the classic poem *The Odyssey* by Homer. It is not a translation of the poem but a story based on the classic writing. It is for the reader who enjoys a story based on classic Greek mythology. I became a lover of Greek mythology when I was eleven years old. *The Odyssey* was one of the first Greek myths I ever read. Since then, I've enjoyed reading and studying Greek mythology whenever I can.

One of the things I discovered about Greek mythology is that there is no single definitive version of a Greek myth. Some interpretations have a darker tone while others are more lighthearted. One writer believes one thing while another believes something else. Most difficult of all, there are endless contradictions concerning any single myth. When writing this story, I reviewed many of these interpretations and took the best from each to create this story. As with any telling, that are some artistic licenses I employed to bring the story to life.

I hope you enjoy this story as much as I did writing it.

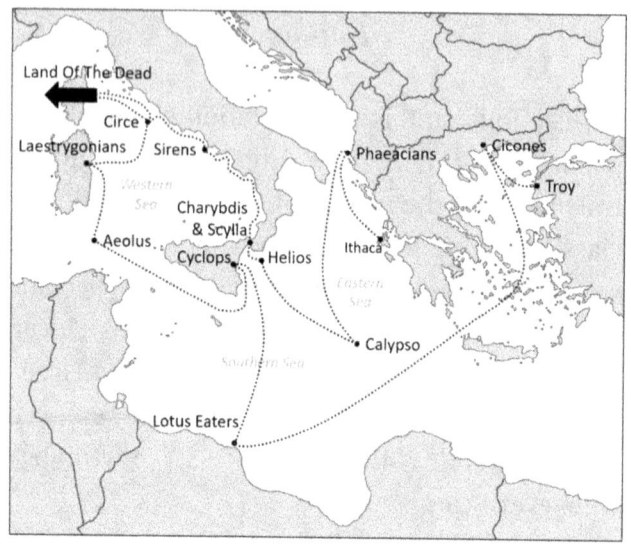

Odysseus's Journey

Table of Contents

CHAPTER 1

THE TROJAN HORSE

It was said he could talk Zeus out of his thunderbolts or sell burial plots to Hades. He was called the great trickster, known for his deception, cleverness, and oratory skills. Some would say he was a sneaky con man who took advantage of the situation. Others, that he was a skilled diplomat who could overcome any situation with his silver tongue. He was wily, intelligent and used brains over brawn whenever he could. His name was Odysseus, King of Ithaca. It was because of his cunning that he and forty other Greeks were here today.

Ithaca was a small island country on the western side of Greece. Being an island country, anyone who lived there were men of the sea. It wasn't as rich and powerful as other countries, but Odysseus was here because of an oath he and the remaining Greeks had taken over a decade ago. Years ago, the Greeks kings were vying for the hand of Helen, the most beautiful woman in Greece. Her father, Tyndareus, refused to let her marry. Her marrying one king would offend the others and risk all-out war. Since Ithaca was a small kingdom, Odysseus realized he didn't stand a chance of winning Helen's hand, so he offered her father a deal. Odysseus wanted to marry Tyndareus's niece Penelope, so he would solve the king's problem if he would support Odysseus's desire to marry Penelope. Tyndareus agreed.

Odysseus had all the Greek kings promise by the Olympians to accept whoever Helen chose as husband. In addition, they vowed to protect and defend Helen and her husband from whoever would do harm to them. They all agreed knowing that if they violated their vow, they would be rendered senseless. Helen chose Menelaus, king of Sparta, to be her husband and, with Tyndareus's support, Odysseus married Penelope. Everyone believed there would be peace throughout the land—peace until the Trojan delegation visited Sparta.

Ten years ago a Trojan delegation visited Sparta on a diplomatic mission. With them was Paris, the son of the Trojan king. When he saw Helen he became enamored with her. The last night of their visit Paris stole Helen away from the Spartan King. When Menelaus found out he called all the Greek kings to honor their oath to protect him and Helen even if it meant going to war.

Odysseus did not wish to go to war. An oracle told him that if a Greek army marched against Troy, the Fates would not allow him to return until he completed a long and difficult voyage filled with pain and sorrow. For this reason he lead a delegation to Troy in an effort to end the dispute through diplomatic means. He offered the Trojans large amounts of land and treasure for the return of Helen but Priam, the king of Troy, would not budge. Thus started the Trojan War.

Before Odysseus sailed, he was visited by his Patron Olympian, Athena. "Odysseus, the Fates have determined that you will return only after a long and difficult voyage. As you know, I cannot go against the Fates, but rest assured, you will return. This war will be difficult for you, your family, your fellow Greeks, the Trojans, and the Olympians. Never forget that no matter how difficult things become, I will always be by your side and will help you whenever I can."

Athena had a lot in common with Odysseus. She admired wisdom, trickery, and deception— skills he had in abundance. He gave her gifts on a regular basis to stay in her good graces. She admired his use of brains over brawn. If something could be done without using brute force, Odysseus was the one who could get the job done.

Over a thousand ships and one hundred thousand Greeks went to war against Troy. Their leader was Agamemnon, Menelaus's brother. He brought the largest contingency of men and ships. The walls of Troy were built by the Olympians Poseidon and Apollo, punishment for rebelling against Zeus years ago. The walls could not be stormed, so the Greeks besieged the city. It was a long and difficult war, and the Greeks would have failed if it hadn't been for Odysseus.

Before the war, it was prophesied the Greeks could not win without their greatest warrior Achilles. Achilles's mother, the Nereid Thetis, knew that if he went to war, he would not return home alive, so she tried to hide him among the servant women. It was Odysseus who exposed the deception and convinced Achilles to join the expedition. Odysseus shook his head with pain when he thought of him. *It was a shame how he died*, Odysseus thought. But Achilles was their greatest warrior, and they would never have won the war without him.

During the war, Odysseus prevented the bulk of the Greek army from withdrawing after Agamemnon foolishly decided to test their determination by allowing them a leave. He also led numerous spying expeditions and prevented the Trojans from spying on the Greek army. He was the one who convinced Achilles to join the fight during a vicious Trojan attack after he refused because of a disagreement he had with Agamemnon. When Helenus told the Greeks Troy would not fall as long as they possessed their Palladium statue, it was Odysseus who led the team that snuck into the city and carried it off. Odysseus wasn't the greatest military strategist, but without him, the Greeks would have surely failed.

After ten years of siege, it was determined that brute force could not take Troy so that left deception, and Odysseus was the man for the job. He realized that the Trojans revered horses above all other animals, so he had his men build a giant wooden horse. The Greek army would pretend to leave Troy in defeat while leaving the horse as a peace offering. A soldier posing as a deserter would also be left behind to convince the Trojans of the story. Inside the horse would be forty Greek soldiers. After the rest of the army left, the Trojans would bring the horse into the city. That night while the Trojans were drunk celebrating their victory, the Greek soldiers would slip out of the horse and open the city gates. That same night the Greek fleet would return, and the army would storm the city.

It was bold and risky. Silence was key to their success. Because of this, the Greeks in the horse did not have armor, and their weapons were wrapped in animal hides to keep them from making noise. Anyone who made a sound would have their throats slit. Hand signals would be used for communication. If the Trojans suspected treachery, they would burn the horse, killing everyone inside.

It was some time after the Greek fleet left before the Trojans came outside their walls to inspect the horse. A great debate ensued. Many of the Trojans wanted to destroy the horse. "Beware of Greeks bearing gifts," they said. Others believed doing so would insult the Olympians since they revered the horse. Laocoön, an Olympian servant, threw a spear against the horse proving it was hollow and warned against accepting it, but two serpents appeared from the ground devouring him. Cassandra, Priam's daughter who was given the gift of prophecy by Apollo, told the Trojans that if they brought the horse in, the Greeks would emerge and destroy them. Unfortunately, Cassandra had spurned Apollo's advances after receiving her gift, so he cursed her that no one would believe her. Odysseus and the rest of the Greeks held their breath during the debate. Finally, it was decided that the horse would be brought into the city.

That evening, the Trojans began a great celebration just as Odysseus predicted. He looked at his fellow Greeks. There were many leaders including Menelaus, Helen's husband. He was in charge of the Spartan contingency, the best soldiers in the Greek army. Menelaus was the second in command, but tonight he knew Odysseus was in charge. This battle required cunning not strength. As the evening wore on, the celebration died down as the Trojans lapsed into a drunken state.

Now was the time to act. Odysseus signaled his men to open the secret hatch and lower the rope so they could exit the wooden horse. Before the last man exited, they lowered their weapons, not that this would have mattered. If the Trojans caught them without their armor, they would be slaughtered. When the last man exited, Odysseus looked around. Just as he predicted, they were just inside the city's main gate. The wooden horse was too large to be brought in one of the smaller gates but not so large as they wouldn't want to bring it inside. It was also large enough so that they wouldn't want to take it very far. Everything was going as planned.

As they made their way to the city gates, Odyssey spotted four guards, all of them in a drunken state from the celebration. Even though they were drunk, it only took one to raise the alarm and the cause would be lost. Odysseus signaled Menelaus, who motioned for four of his men. With the stealth of a morning mist, all four Spartans snuck up on the guards and slit their throats. Next he signaled Menelaus to have his men take a defensive position. The rest of the Greeks slowly opened the main gates.

Now was the most dangerous time. If the Trojans noticed the gates were open, they would send a contingent to investigate. The Spartans were the best soldiers, but they couldn't hold off the Trojan army forever. Eventually, they would break through and slaughter everyone. That was why he then positioned his men so that if something went wrong, they could demolish the gate's mechanism. Hopefully, this would keep the Trojans from closing the gates.

Fortunately, it didn't come to that. The Greek army returned and rushed through the open gates. Their war cries were terrifying as they slaughtered the Trojans. The fires would light the skies as the sack of Troy began.

The Greeks weren't the only ones watching Troy. On Mount Olympus, The Greek Olympians had also become involved in the war. Aphrodite, Artemis, Apollo, and Ares supported the Trojans while Poseidon, Athena, Hera, Hephaestus, and Hermes supported the Greeks. In the middle was Zeus, King of the Olympians. He was supposedly neutral, but in reality he supported the Trojans though he dared not show it.

The Trojan War became so divisive that the Olympians became actively involved during the conflict. The fact was the Olympians were dangerously close to starting a civil war, a war that would be disastrous for the entire world. Once the war was over, Zeus did everything he could to end the rife and bring the Olympians back together. Even though his side lost, he was more interested in preserving the peace on Mount Olympus. Of all the Olympians, none were happier for a Greek victory than Poseidon and Athena.

Poseidon was the Olympian of the sea. He also hated of the Trojans. Years ago, Hera, Poseidon, and Apollo lead a revolt against their younger brother Zeus, King of the Olympians. They failed. As part of his punishment, Poseidon was forced to be a Trojan slave and build the walls of Troy. Poseidon always resented this punishment and wanted to see them destroyed for that humiliation. In addition, the Greeks were seafarers, so they held a special place in his heart.

Athena was the Olympian of wisdom and of war. She resented the Trojans for the slight Trojan prince Paris gave her just before he ran off with Helen. She also admired the strategy and deception involved in warfare and not the vicious bloodshed and violence her brother Ares enjoyed. Above all else she admired Odysseus. He was the best example of the traits she admired most in a commander.

The cooperation between Athena and Poseidon during the Trojan War was something that shocked the other Olympians. Before the war, they were bitter rivals. Their dispute arose when the citizens of Athens chose Athena to be their patron Olympian over Poseidon. This infuriated Poseidon. At one point, he raised his trident to do battle with Athena, a challenge she was more than willing to accept. Only a thunderbolt from Zeus separated them, preventing a titanic battle that would have ravaged Earth. Since then, Poseidon exacted his revenge against Athena through other means.

With the Greek victory, Poseidon and Athena looked at each other and smiled. They were happy but would never gloat and risk Zeus's wrath. Zeus was Athena's father and Poseidon's younger brother. Even though they were family, defying Zeus could bring dire sequences as Poseidon had found out after his attempted revolt. Now was the time to end the division and bring the Olympians back together.

Now was the time for healing.

CHAPTER 2

RAID ON THE CICONS

O dysseus was standing on the shore as his ships were readying to sail for Ithaca. A week had passed since the sacking of Troy, and its smoldering ruins could still be seen from miles away.

"Well, Odysseus," a familiar voice said, "it will be good to be back home."

Odysseus turned to see Agamemnon, their leader. "Yes, sir. It's been a long time since I've seen my wife and son. It will be good to see them again." It had been ten years since any of them had seen their families. It had been a long war, a war that had cost them dearly. Achilles, Ajax, and many others died returning Helen to Menelaus.

Agamemnon took stock in Odysseus. He had kept the army together and come up with a plan to bring the war to an end. "I've sent heralds ahead. Everyone will know the war is over, and we are on our way back."

"Thank you, sir," Odysseus responded. As the two men continued, another man approached.

"Sire, the ships are loaded, and we're ready to sail."

Odysseus turned. It was Eurylochus, his second-in-command and brother-in-law. Odysseus did not care much for him. He wasn't much of a soldier; some would say he was a coward. He was always complaining and stirring up trouble. He had married Odysseus's sister which is why he was his second-in-command, but Odysseus did not count on him much. When this expedition was over, he could finally rid himself of Eurylochus.

"Thank you, Eurylochus," Odysseus replied. "Tell the men we set sail in an hour. Anyone not on board will be left behind." Ithaca's contribution was small—only twelve ships and six hundred men. Odysseus, however, was proud of the fact that in ten years of warfare, he had not lost a single man.

As Eurylochus left, Odysseus returned to his conversation with Agamemnon. "Well, sir, it has been a pleasure serving you."

"You've been a great help and a valuable asset. Fair winds and good sailing for you, Odysseus." The two men shook hands and then departed.

As Odysseus boarded his ship, he was greeted by Polites. "Is everyone on board?" he asked.

"Yes, sire. I have personally counted, and everyone is present and accounted for." Polites was his friend and confidant, and he trusted him without question. If Odysseus asked for something to be done, Polites would get it done.

"Then let's make sail while the wind is with us," Odysseus commanded. All Greek ships had a sail, and it was used whenever possible. If the wind wasn't right, the men rowed.

Their return trip started out fine with a good tail wind to carry them home, but it didn't last long. A storm appeared and blew their ships off course to the North. When it ended two days later, they were on an unfamiliar shore.

"Eurylochus," Odysseus said, "take a scouting party and find out where we are."

Next, he turned to Polites. "Check out the ships and see if there is any damage."

Polites was the first to return. "Sire, a few ships have some minor damage. It won't take them long to repair. Unfortunately, we've lost most of our grain."

"Thank you," he replied.

An hour later, Eurylochus returned. "Sire, we've found several natives. It appears we have landed near the city of Ismara, stronghold of the

Cicons. It also appears they are in the middle of a festival, and there are few men in the city."

Odysseus knew he had an opportunity. Cicons had been an ally of Troy during the war. They supplied the city with grain and fought the Greeks several time. They were tough fighters and a resourceful people. If it weren't for the grain situation, Odysseus would have left right away to avoid them.

He turned to Eurylochus. "Ready the men for battle. If we strike hard and fast, we can take the grain and be gone before the Cicon men return." Then he leaned in to close to Eurylochus. "Keep control of the men. If they begin looting, we could be surprised and find ourselves on the receiving end of a Ciconian attack."

"Yes, sire," Eurylochus replied.

Next Odysseus turned to Polites. "Take fifty well-armed men with you to guard the ships, and be ready in case there is trouble."

Thirty minutes later, the Greeks were on the move. Before long, they reached Ismara.

"Charge!" Odysseus yelled as the soldiers attacked the city. The Ciconians were taken by surprise. The men who resisted were slaughtered, and the city was overrun. Even though they were surprised, the people were beginning to put up a strong resistance. If they didn't win soon, Odysseus could start losing men.

It was during the battle that Odysseus heard a voice. "Stop! Please in the name of the Olympians stop!"

Odysseus turned to see an old man with several servants standing in a temple. "You are an ally of Troy," he yelled. "You deserve your fate."

"I am Maron, servant of Apollo," the old man said. "It is true that we were enemies, but Troy has been taken, and the war is over. Please, take what you need from the city and stop the slaughter."

"Why should I stop when I can take what we need."

"Because if you do, I will provide you with several skins of Ciconian wine. And I will order the resistance to end."

Odysseus was intrigued. Not only were Ciconians skilled fighters, but they made the best wine in the Mediterranean—a valuable prize indeed. He considered taking the wine, but storming an Olympian's sanctuary would only bring down their wrath—something he wanted to avoid.

"Agreed," Odysseus replied. And with that, he ordered an end to the attack. As promised, Maron ordered all resistance to end. Odysseus took ten men to carry the wine and some grain back to the ships.

As Odysseus looked around, a strange feeling overcame him. He turned to Eurylochus. "Have half the men gather as much grain as they can. Have the other half take as much loot as they can carry. We'll divide it up equally when we reach the ships. Make only one trip. I want to be gone as quickly as I can."

Eurylochus looked at him with a puzzled look. "Sire, why should we deny the men their prize?"

"The Ciconians gave in too easily," Odysseus said. "I don't like this. Something's wrong. Now make haste, and let's be gone before anything happens." As he was leaving, Odysseus noticed that one of Maron's servants had left. No, he didn't like this at all.

Several hours had passed, and the rest of his crew had not returned. Odysseus was becoming concerned. "Continue loading the ships," he told Polites. "I'm going to see what's taking Eurylochus so long." As he left, he gave his friend one last command. "When you're finished, have the men form ranks and be ready for battle, just in case there's trouble."

As Odysseus approached Ismara, he heard a wild commotion coming from the city. To his horror, he saw his men running amuck, drunk, and looting the town. "Eurylochus!" he cried. "What are you doing? I told you to collect as much grain and loot as you can carry then return to the ships. Not let the men run wild!"

"Sire," he replied in a casual manner, "the men have won a great victory! Let them enjoy this time. They've earned it."

Odysseus was furious. "Only a small portion of the men were in the city, and we have no idea where the rest of them are. Get control of the men. We have to leave!"

Eurylochus was about to say something when they heard trumpets blow. It was as Odysseus feared. The Ciconian men had returned and were attacking their disorganized and drunken troops. They were attacking from the north with Maron and his servants showing them the way. Odysseus organized some of the men into a defense to slow them down, but there were just too many. He watched as several of his men were cut down. Odysseus organized a fighting retreat too, but he was losing men at an alarming rate. Suddenly there came Ciconian attack from the west. They were trying to cut them off from their ships. If they succeeded, Odysseus and his men would be destroyed.

"Eurylochus!" he cried. "Take some men and protect our left!" But Eurylochus was as confused and disorganized as his men. If things weren't bad enough, Odysseus heard more trumpets from the west. All seemed lost when Odysseus saw that these new troop weren't Ciconian troops but Greek soldiers. It was Polites and the men he left to guard the ships. He had heard the battle and rushed to help his king. It wasn't a very large force, but it was enough to sow confusion among the Ciconians and allow the Greeks to escape.

As the Greeks approached the ships, Odysseus discovered that Polites had left some of the men to make the ships ready to sail. The Greeks hastily boarded the ships and set sail just as the Ciconian troops reached the shore. As they rowed away, they could hear the Ciconians jeering and cursing them.

"It appears the Greeks came down with a case of victory disease," Zeus commented. Zeus was watching Odysseus's return with great interest. A crafty mortal who defeated his enemies with guile instead of force always attracted the attention of the Olympian King.

"Yes, Brother, they did," Poseidon replied, "but their commander sensed the trap and tried to prevent it from happening. If his second-in-command had been more attentive and restrained the men, the attack wouldn't have happened."

"He did save his men once the attack began," Athena added.

Zeus looked at both of them as he sat on his throne. "He is still the commander and responsible for whatever happens to his men. It should never have happened." Then he stood. "Let's see if this mortal is as crafty as you think he is."

Athena gave Poseidon a concerned look. The tasks her father came up with to test mortals could be far deadlier than his thunderbolts. It didn't help that Odysseus was the one who came up with the plan that defeated the Trojans. As Zeus raised his hand, Athena hoped Odysseus was ready for whatever was coming next.

CHAPTER 3

THE LOTUS EATERS

"Sire, we've completed the count," Polites said. "We lost seventy-two men."

Odysseus nodded. In ten years of fighting, he hadn't lost a single man, but one act of hubris from his men cost them seventy-two people. No excuse. It was Eurylochus who let the men run wild, but he was the commander. Ultimate responsibility fell on his shoulders. He was about to say something when a strong wind from the north arose, blowing his ships south. For nine days the wind blew, but on the morning of the tenth day, it suddenly stopped. Odysseus and his men found themselves on the coast of an unknown shore.

Everything looked peaceful. He turned to his second-in-command. "Eurylochus, have the men go ashore, rest, and prepare a warm meal. Then have them gather as much supplies as possible." Next, he turned to three of his men.

"Go inland and scout the area. See who lives here and what kind of people they are."

The three men left. Later, as his men cooked their meals, Odysseus became concerned that the three scouts hadn't returned. "Eurylochus, our scouts haven't returned. Keep the men close to shore as they gather supplies. I'm going to go search for the missing scouts."

"Yes, sire," Eurylochus replied.

As Odysseus moved inland, he found a path and followed it. Soon he found a city where the citizens appeared to be having a festival. As he approached, he noticed the citizens enjoying all types of pleasure. There was drinking, feasting, singing, dancing, and other sorts of merriment that staggered Odysseus's mind. Many were engaged in the pleasures of the flesh as well. These people didn't seem to have a care in the world. As he entered the city, a large well-dressed man approached him.

"Welcome, stranger!" the man said with a gleeful expression. "Come and accept our hospitality!"

"What place is this?" Odysseus asked.

The man smiled. "I'm not sure. I think this is the island of Djerba."

"What's the name of this city?"

The man just smiled. "I'm not sure. No one's ever called it anything but home."

"Who's in charge?"

Again, another smile. "I don't know. Me, maybe, or no one. We all love it here. The weather's perfect, and there's plenty of wine. We want for nothing." At his last comment, the man just laughed as if he were in a drunken state. Then he handed Odysseus a strange looking fruit.

"What's this?" Odysseus asked.

"It's the lotus fruit," the man replied. "It grows everywhere. It tastes divine."

Odysseus looked around. Everyone seemed to be eating the lotus fruit. *Strange*, he thought. *This seems to be all they're eating.* "Where are the cattle, sheep, or goats?" he asked someone.

"There aren't any."

"What about fish?"

"None of that either. Here take the lotus fruit—it's very good."

Odysseus politely refused the fruit and continued on. The people seemed friendly, he thought. No ill will or animosity. Everywhere he went, people were in some kind of dreamlike state, like they didn't have a care in the world. Most important of all, they respected the ancient custom of hospitality. A custom that was very important to the Olympians, especially Zeus.

Under the rules of hospitality, hosts were expected to provide visitors with food, shelter, a bath, gifts, and a safe night and then escort them to their next destination. The visitors were expected to behave, be courteous to their host, not pose a threat, and provide the same favors for any visitors who showed up at their homes. In the house of Odysseus, even beggars were granted hospitality.

But something wasn't right. That man over there appeared to be Egyptian, and the man he was talking to was Libyan. Those two cultures hated each other, so these two men shouldn't even be in the same room much less having a conversation. Not long afterwards, he found his men celebrating with the others. As he got closer, he was shocked to see that they were with were Trojans. Trojans! A few weeks ago, they were trying to kill each other. Now they were celebrating together? He was about to intervene but then stopped himself. Something was not right, and he had to find out what.

He approached another man. "If this is an island, where is the harbor?" he asked.

"Harbor?" the man said through his dreamy haze. "We don't have one."

"I see different cultures here, cultures that hated each other."

The man had a puzzled look on his fate. "Hate each other? No one hates anyone here. We live in peace and harmony." Then he handed Odysseus some lotus fruit. "Here, accept our hospitality and have some lotus fruit."

Again, Odysseus politely refused and moved on. A few minutes later, he came across another man who looked Ethiopian. "Where are you from?" he asked.

"Where am I from? I don't really know." Then he laughed a silly laugh. "From here, of course." He also tried to hand Odysseus some of the lotus fruit.

For the next couple of hours, it was the same thing over and over again. Everyone was in a euphoric state, no one remembered where they were from, and all of them were eating the lotus fruit. Try as he might, he could not get at straight answer from these people. No one seemed to care about anything—not their home, friends, or the outside world. Only celebrating and eating the lotus fruit.

Odysseus reached the other side of town. He was about to return when he noticed something in the tall grass. As he approached, it looked like a homemade tent, a shelter for someone who didn't want to live in town. As he searched the dwelling, he found some papyrus with writing in Greek. As he read it, he realized it was from the Caption of a Greek merchant ship. As Odysseus read the papyrus, he realized it told the story about what happened to them.

My crew and I were shipwrecked here several months ago, it began. *These strange people cared nothing about their homes and lived in a dreamlike state. All they ate was the lotus fruit. There was no livestock, wild game in the fields, or fish in the water. No other fruits or vegetables grew on their island, only the lotus fruit.*

Some of my crew accepted their hospitality, ate the lotus fruit, and forgot their homes and loved ones. They entered the same dreamlike state that these people lived in and cared nothing about returning to their homes. Before long, our food ran out. Then one by one my men gave into hunger and began eating the lotus fruit. I am the last one left, and I can't hold out much longer.

As Odysseus continued reading, the Captain's final words sent a chill down his spine. *Leave this accursed island while you can or you will suffer the same fate as me and my crew.*

Odysseus dropped the writing and ran back to his ships. When he reached them, he saw his crew loading fresh water and other supplies onto the ships including the lotus fruit.

"Eurylochus! Have the men throw that fruit overboard!" He then explained what was going on and the dangers of the strange fruit. Next, he looked at three of his best troops. "Lycaon, Amphialos, and Alkimos, suit up in full armor. We're going to retrieve our comrades." The four left and forced his men who had eaten the lotus fruit back onto the ships.

"No, sire," they pleaded. "Let us stay! This is paradise!" But Odysseus would not listen. He was taking them back to their homes and loved ones no matter how much they begged to stay.

When they returned, Odysseus issued his orders. "Eurylochus, make the ships ready to sail. We're leaving this cursed island!" Then he had Eurylochus tied the three scouts to the decks so that the lotus infected men wouldn't try to leave and rejoin the lotus-eaters. They were to stay there until the effects of the fruit wore off if they ever did.

"Well, Brother" Poseidon said, "Odysseus discovered the trap and avoided it."

"Yes, he did," Zeus replied. "This Greek is more clever than I gave him credit."

Athena was happy as well. "Please don't distress father," she said. "Odysseus is a clever one. Yes, he has made mistakes but he is one to learn from them." She knew better than to antagonize her father, otherwise he would come up with a task that no mortal could ever escape, not even one as clever as Odysseus.

Zeus smiled at his daughter. "Do not fret, daughter. I just wanted to see how clever this mortal was. To avoid the lotus-eaters takes a man with a sharp mind that is quick to recognize danger in its most subtle form. A clever man indeed."

Poseidon and Athena were pleased Odysseus passed Zeus's test. "See what I told you, Uncle," Athena said. "Odysseus is one of the cleverest people in Greece. Not many would have taken the time to figure out the real danger of the lotus-eaters."

"Yes, he is," Poseidon said. "He's from Ithaca, so he's a seafarer as well. We'll keep an eye on him and make sure he returns home."

"Yes, he has been away a long time, and he looks forward to seeing his wife and family."

"As long he doesn't do anything foolish, he should make it back without incident."

CHAPTER 4

THE CYCLOPS

Ten days after leaving the lotus-eaters, the Greeks come upon an unknown island. With their supplies running low, Odysseus ordered his men to make landfall. On the island, they found wild goats and sheep. They hunted the game, feasted, and replenished their supplies. The next morning, Odysseus set out to discover who lived on this island.

"Eurylochus, gather Lycaon, Amphialos, Alkimos, Amphidamas, Antilochus, and six others," he ordered. "We're going find who lives on this island." Just as they were about to leave, Odysseus looked at his men. "Lycaon, Antilochus, bring one of the Ciconian wineskins. We may need it as a gift for the residents."

They made their way to the top of a hill where they found a path leading inland. As they traveled, they saw large flocks of sheep and goats but no shepherds. *Odd*, Odysseus thought. *This many animals and no shepherds?*

The path was easy to travel and led them to the top of another hill where they found a large cave. Inside, the Greeks found large amounts of cheese and various meats. They began to indulge themselves when Alkimos cried out, "Sire, over here."

As the group approached, they found a large stone axe and club, over twice as large as any one of them. "Sire," Eurylochus said with a nervous voice, "I do not like this. We should take what we can, return to our ships and leave this island."

Odysseus considered this but thought differently. "All creatures were governed by the rules of hospitality, including the owner of this cave," he said. "If they violate this rule, they risk the wrath of the Olympians. We shall stay and see what manner of person lives here."

As night approached, all different types of sheep and goats entered the cave. Then the owner entered, a huge creature five times larger than any one of them. He stood like a man but was dirty with unkempt hair and dressed in animal skins. He appeared almost human except for his face. Instead of two eyes, he had only the one single eye in middle of his forehead. After his flocks had entered, he rolled a huge stone in front of the cave's entrance. Then he started a fire and milked several of his flock. Afterwards, he drank the milk and ate some cheese. After finishing his supper, he turned and saw the Greeks.

"Who are you and what are you doing in my home?" he asked.

Although he was terrified, Odysseus stepped forward to address the creature. In a calm voice, he said, "We are Greeks returning home from a long voyage."

"Greeks," he replied. "I have heard of such people but have never met one." Then he sat down and continued his conversation. "From where do you hail, Greek?"

"We are returning from a war in a faraway land in the east."

"From Troy?" the creature asked. Odysseus nodded. The creature continued. "If indeed you are returning from that war, tell me more about your adventures."

Since the creature seemed interested, Odysseus told the creature the tale about their ten-year struggle with Troy. As he finished his tale, he asked the creature. "By what name may I call our gracious host."

"My name is Polyphemus. Tell me, Greek, where are the rest of your companions and ships?"

Odysseus became suspicious at this question. He feared the creature was trying to find out if there were more of them and where they were, so he used cunning to create a story. "We are alone, Polyphemus. Our ships ran into a storm, and we were separated from our comrades. The storm drove our ships into the rocks, and now we are shipwrecked on your island."

"How did you find my cave?"

"With great difficulty," Odysseus began. "There was no markings or path where we came ashore. We traveled through rough terrain and climbed a large hill and found your home. We came inside to rest just before you returned."

The creature seemed to believe Odysseus's story. It was then that Odysseus continued. "Oh, wise Polyphemus, we simple travelers request you follow the rules of hospitality set forth by the Olympians and help us on our way. We need your help to continue our journey. Please help us and not risk the wrath of the Olympians."

The creature leaned back and began to laugh. "Stranger, you are a fool who does not understand this land or our ways. We are descendants of the great cyclopes Brontes, Steropes, and Arges, brothers of the Titians who helped the Olympians defeat them in war. We do not honor the rules of hospitality, nor do we fear the Olympians!"

Suddenly the cyclops seized two of Odysseus's men. Then he bashed their heads against the rocks, pulled a stone knife, carved them up, and ate them as the rest watched helplessly.

After his grizzly feast, the cyclops spoke again. "You Greeks are tougher than the Phoenician travelers that have passed this way," he said. Then he mockingly addressed Odysseus. "Thank you for your hospitality. It's been a long time since I've had such delicacies. I will greatly enjoy them for a long time." Then he laughed, prepared his bed, and went to sleep.

Shock and horror gripped Odysseus and his men. They had seen all manners of death during their war with Troy: men who had been hacked with swords, crushed by clubs, and burned alive in fires. Nothing—absolutely nothing—could prepare them for what they had just seen. Their comrades, who were alive just minutes ago, were murdered then butchered like cattle right before their eyes. Their remains were used for this monster's grotesque meal. Each man realized they could be the next one devoured whenever this beast became hungry. They were brave warriors, but this atrocity crushed their hearts and sank their spirits. Hopelessness overcame them as they realized their fate.

Odysseus was incensed. He pulled his sword and started toward the cyclops only to have his men stop him. "No, sire," Lycaon whispered. "If you do slay the beast then we will all die the slow death of starvation because he is the only one who can move the stone that blocks our escape. If you try and fail, he will surely devour you." Odysseus looked at the stone. Lycaon was right. Even with all their shipmates, they could never move it. In addition, there was no way to know how many cyclopes lived on the island, so the longer they delayed, the less likely they and their shipmates would survive. Brute force would not save them. Only cunning and trickery would.

As he looked into his men's eyes, Odysseus saw terror and fear. "Look," he said, "we are going to survive this. I have a plan. It will be costly, but we will escape."

The next morning Polyphemus awoke and devoured two more of Odysseus`s men. Then he rolled the great stone away from the entrance and drove his flocks out. As he left, he rolled the great stone back in front of the entrance trapping them inside. Odysseus began to issue orders.

"Eurylochus, take Lycaon, Amphialos, Alkimos, and Amphidamas and carve a large pole from the cyclops's club. Make sure to sharpen one end. Antilochus, start a fire. The rest of you look through the monster's things and find the largest bowl you can. Hurry! We must be finished before he returns." His men did as they were ordered. When the pole was finished, they thrust the sharpened end into the fire to harden it. The pole was so large it took six men to lift it. When they were finished, they put out the fire then hid the pole and large bowl they found. They completed their tasks just as the cyclops returned with his flocks.

The cyclops moved the great stone, drove his flocks into the cave, and then returned it to the opening. As Polyphemus had done the night before, he milked his flocks and ate some cheese. Once again, he devoured two more of Odysseus`s men. After he finished his gruesome meal, Odysseus approached him.

"Great Polyphemus, since you are not accustomed to the acts of hospitality, let us show you its greatness by asking you to accept a humble gift of ours."

"Gift?" the cyclops asked. "What gift could you possibly offer me?"

Odysseus signaled his men. They brought out the large bowl they found and handed it to the cyclops.

The cyclops saw a strange liquid in it. "What is it?" he asked.

"It's called wine. Ciconian wine to be exact. The best anywhere."

Polyphemus looked at the wine and smelled it. Then, after a quick glance to make sure the great stone was in place, drank. Odysseus could tell from his expression the beast liked it. He handed the bowl back. "More."

"More for our host!" Odysseus cried. His men quickly filled the bowl and handed it back.

Polyphemus drank it just as quickly as the first. "More," he demanded. The Greeks quickly filled his bowl. Before long, the wine was having the desired effect—the cyclops was becoming drunk. The more he drank, the drunker he became. The more he drank, the more the Greeks cheered him on. It was as if they were at a celebration. It was during his drunken state that Polyphemus addressed Odysseus.

"Tell me, stranger. What is your name?"

"Nobody," Odysseus replied.

"Well, Nobody, I will grant you hospitality," Polyphemus said with a drunken smile. "I will eat you last!" Then he laughed a large, loud drunken laugh as he struggled to remain on his feet. He held out his bowl. "More!" he demanded.

Before long, the cyclops was lying on his back completely drunk. "More," he struggled to say. After his last bowl of wine, he passed out. With the cyclops passed out, he would not be a threat as the Greeks put the second part of their plan into action.

Odysseus had his men retrieve the sharpened pole they made. Then, with every man holding the pole, the Greeks ran as fast as they could and, with all their might, thrust the sharpened end into the single eye of the monster. Polyphemus howled with pain as he pulled the pole from his eye. "Nobody, you have blinded me!" he screamed. "I will devour you all for this!"

Odysseus and his men easily avoided the blind monster as he flailed around his cave trying to catch them. He screamed in pain with each movement he made and yelled obscenities at the Greeks. He was making such a commotion that the other cyclops rushed to his cave to see what was happening.

"Polyphemus, what is happening?" they yelled with great concern.

"Nobody has blinded me!" he cried.

The other cyclops turned to each other. "Polyphemus, either you are dreaming, or you have offended the Olympians and they are punishing you." With that they left.

Polyphemus tried all night to catch the Greeks but failed. As morning arose, he gave up, removed the great stone, and sat at the entrance. He was allowing his flocks to go out and graze, but when something tried to leave, the cyclops would feel their tops to make sure it wasn't a

Greek trying to escape. If Greeks tried to escape, he would catch and devour them.

Odysseus was ready for this. As the flocks started to leave, he tied three sheep together then tied one of his men under each group. As the group left the cave, the cyclops would feel the tops of the sheep but not the man hiding underneath. All of his men made their escape. As for himself, he found the largest ram, crawled under it, and held onto its underside. He planned on making his escape when the ram left the cave.

As his ram started to leave, Polyphemus felt its back and stopped it. "Tell me, oh ram of mine," he asked, "where are the Greeks so that I may capture them?" Odysseus held his breath waiting to see what would happen. When the ram didn't answer, he let it pass.

Once outside the cave, Odysseus let go of the ram and untied his men. They quickly ran to their ships. "Make ready to sail!" he yelled. "There are monsters on this island, and we must leave now!" The Greeks stopped whatever they were doing and made their ships ready to sail.

Polyphemus heard Odysseus and realized he and his men had escaped. In his blind state, he stumbled and groped his way toward the beach. He reached the top of the hill just as the Greeks were rowing away. "Nobody!" he screamed.

After everything he had been through since landing on the island, Odysseus could not resist the temptation to taunt Polyphemus. "What's the matter, cyclops?" he yelled. "Having trouble seeing us?"

Polyphemus heard the taunt and threw a large boulder at his ship. It fell short because the Greeks were too far away.

"Nice try, cyclops! Maybe if you had two eyes instead of one you could still see and find us!"

A dejected Polyphemus lay on the beach and cried out, "Nobody, I shall call on my father to punish you for what you did to me. You shall feel his wrath and wish you were never born."

Odysseus laughed. Then he yelled, "Call your wretched father or whatever beast spawned you, cyclops! Just remember to tell them that it wasn't Nobody who blinded you. It was Odysseus!"

The last thing Odysseus and his men heard as they left the island was Polyphemus's muttered cry, "Oh father, hear my plea, pleases take vengeance on Odysseus for blinding me and insulting your name."

Zeus sat on his on throne on Mount Olympus as he and the other Olympians listened to Poseidon`s scream and rant his grievances against the Greeks.

"Justice! Revenge! Vengeance!" he shouted. "First Odysseus blinds my son and then he insults me! No mortal has the right to maim an Olympian's son or insult them. I demand vengeance and revenge against Odysseus!"

Athena couldn't believe Odysseus could be so foolish. She didn't agree with everything Poseidon said, but she could not go against him. She and the other Olympians thought Polyphemus was a brute and the world would be better off without him even if he was Poseidon`s son. He had violated the rules of hospitality which none of the Olympians condoned. He also ate Odysseus`s men. Cannibalism was an act so repugnant to the Olympians they might have punished Polyphemus on their own. He would have eaten all of them if Odysseus hadn't escaped, and if escaping meant blinding the cyclops, then so be it.

But insulting an Olympian is something none of them would tolerate, not even herself. That cost Odysseus the support of the remaining Olympians, even the ones who did not like Poseidon or Polyphemus. None of the other Olympians would stand for such insults, so she had to appear to support Poseidon`s claim. That way she could bide her time and help him at a later date.

The worst part was that Odysseus would have gotten away with it if he hadn't told Polyphemus his real name. That was foolish. The cyclops could not ask for vengeance or revenge if he didn't know who blinded him or insulted his father. Without knowing his real name, there was nothing Poseidon could have done to him. Zeus would never allow an Olympian to randomly punish someone because he had been wronged. He had to know the transgressor's true name. No name, no revenge.

"Poseidon is right, father," Athena said. "No Olympian should suffer such insults." This caught the other Olympians off guard. They all knew she was Odysseus's Patron Olympian and were surprised she spoke against him, especially since she and Poseidon were rivals in every aspect short of the Trojan War. Athena knew if she came to Odysseus's aid after such indignities against an Olympian, she would lose the support of the rest. She had to appear to support her uncle until she could help Odysseus another time. If that meant Odysseus had to suffer her uncle's wrath, there was nothing she could do about it.

But all was not lost for Odysseus. Poseidon was arrogant, brash, violent, and quick to anger. His temper and behavior aggravated the other Olympians, so their support for him would soon fall away. She also knew that Poseidon's revolt against Zeus was fresh in her father's mind. He would keep his older brother on a short leash. Athena could also help Odysseus in other subtle ways that her uncle wouldn't notice.

Zeus began to speak. "No Olympian must endure the insults Odysseus has done to Poseidon. You may have your vengeance, Brother." Then he rose and pointed at Poseidon. "But mark my words, Brother. The Fates have decreed that Odysseus shall return to Ithaca, so you cannot smite him. Only the Fates can know when a mortal will die. If you get them to change their predictions, that's between you and them, but you cannot strike him down!"

At least father didn't condemn Odysseus's actions against Polyphemus, Athena thought. That was a small victory. Then she shook her head. *Oh Odysseus, why did you have to tell Polyphemus your name.*

CHAPTER 5

AEOLUS

O dysseus took stock of their situation as they pulled away from the island of the cyclops. He had lost six more men—men who died a horrible death. It could have been a lot worse. If the rest of the cyclopes had found their ships, they all would be dead. He made a mistake staying in the cave instead in of leaving right away, something he knew Eurylochus was whispering to the men. He was also worried about Lycaon, Amphialos, Alkimos, Amphidamas, and Antilochus. While they had survived the horrors of the cyclops, it was clear they were traumatized by the event. Hopefully they would recover once they returned home. The only good news was that the three men who had eaten the lotus fruit had recovered their senses.

Odysseus was about to set a course from home when a great storm arose. For four days, the winds blew them west, away from Ithaca into the unknown Western Sea. The strong winds battered their ships. When the winds stopped, they found themselves in front of an island with cliffs so high and shear no man could ever climb them. On top of the cliffs was a city surrounded by walls of unbreakable bronze. The island was floating, constantly moving so that it would never be in the same place twice. After circling the island, they found a harbor where they could dock their ship.

Once they docked their ships, a well-dressed man with his attendants approached them. "Welcome to Aeolia," he said. "I am Aeolus, keeper of the winds."

Every sailor including Odysseus knew who Aeolus was. He was an immortal, a being not as powerful as an Olympian, but someone who needed to be respected and feared. Aeolus controlled the winds, so every sailor tried to stay on his good side so that he would give them fair tail winds on their journeys.

Odysseus stepped forward, bowed, and then addressed his host. "I am Odysseus, king of Ithaca. We are on our way home from the Trojan War, but foul winds have driven us into the Western Sea."

Aeolus nodded. "The war in the east," he said. "I have heard of it. The great conflict that even divided the Olympians on Mount Olympus. A violent one indeed." Then he looked at Odysseus`s ships. "Your ships need repair Odysseus. Come, accept our hospitality while you repair your ships. You can tell us about you deeds during your stay."

That evening, Odysseus and his men were treated to a feast in their honor while Odysseus told his host of their deeds during the war. Aeolus was a gracious host giving the Greeks everything they needed to repair and resupply their ships. After a month, they were ready to sail. As Odysseus was prepared to thank his host and say his final farewell, Aeolus approached him and said, "Follow me, Odysseus, there's one more thing I can do for you."

He led Odysseus to the top of a hill where two of his attendants were standing. They were holding a large leather bag. Aeolus started an incantation that caused the winds to rush into the bag. When he finished, his attendants closed the bag and tied it tightly. Aeolus handed Odysseus the bag. "As your host, the rules of hospitality require that I assist you onto your next destination. Your fastest way home is through the Southern Sea, but those winds are dangerous. Inside this bag are all the foul winds that will keep you from returning home. Only a gentle westerly wind will be left which will take you home. As long as you do not open the bag before you dock your ships, you will return home safely."

"But beware, Odysseus," he warned, "there are two conditions to this gift. First, you must release the winds by the evening of the second night after you return. If you don't, a storm will arise and destroy your kingdom. Second, you cannot tell anyone what is in the bag. That way any Olympian who wishes to use them is not offended. If you tell anyone, the winds will release and sink your ships."

Odysseus thanked Aeolus for the gift and returned to his ships. As he boarded, his men noticed the large bag he was carrying. "Sire, the ships are ready to sail," Eurylochus reported. Then he asked, "What's in the bag, sire?"

Odysseus ignored his question. "Set sail for home, Eurylochus." Then he took the bag with him to the front of the ship and guarded it.

Odysseus guarded the bag so closely that he refused to sleep. After three days, Eurylochus began spreading rumors. "I tell you our king is deceiving us. Aeolus gave us no treasure, but Odysseus arrived with a large bag and won't tell us what's in it. At Ismara, he told us to share our loot with him, but he won't share with us what's in his bag! He guards it so closely he won't even sleep. I tell you it's treasure, and our King wishes to keep it for himself." For days, Eurylochus spread his rumors and lies about Odysseus.

On the seventh day, there was great joy on the ships. They were within sight of Ithaca. They were almost home. A great cheer arose from the ships. An exhausted Odysseus looked up from the bow of his ship. He could see his home. In a few hours, their journey would be over. "We're almost home men!" he cried. "We're almost home."

Odysseus wasn't the only one watching. For days, Poseidon had been trying to raise a storm against the Greeks, but for some reason he couldn't. Then he realized that somehow Odysseus had captured the winds. Without them, there would be no storm.

His anger and rage could be felt throughout Mount Olympus. He soon realized that the bag he was guarding must be carrying the winds. He also heard the rumblings of Eurylochus. If he could only get the Greeks to open the bag. Then he came up with a clever plan. He may not have the winds, but he still controlled the currents and tides. He began gently rocking Odysseus's ship back and forth with the ocean currents.

It was more than Odysseus could take. After being awake for seven days, the gentle rocking caused him to fall asleep. When Eurylochus saw this, he made his move. He convinced the disturbed Lycaon, Amphialos, Alkimos, Amphidamas, and Antilochus to steal the bag and bring it to him. Then he took it to the back of the boat and opened it for everyone to see. In an instant, violent winds escaped and began to blow. Thirty-foot waves started crashing over the sides, wrecking deck boards and snapping masts.

Odysseus woke to the commotion. "What have you done!" he yelled. He turned to look back at Ithaca only to see it fade away in the distance. For ten days, the winds blew the fleet west away from Ithaca. When they stopped, Odysseus found himself at the island of Aeolia. His ships were wrecked and in desperate need of repairs. This time when they entered the harbor, there was no greeting party, only silence.

"Wait here," Odysseus told his crew. "I will go and see Aeolus."

Odysseus walked inland and found the keeper of the winds eating dinner with his family. He looked up at Odysseus with a puzzled look on his face. "Why have you returned Odysseus, King of Ithaca?"

"Sire, we humbly ask for your help one more time. We were in sight of our homeland when sleep overtook me. My men stole the bag of winds and, thinking it was treasure, opened it. Violent winds blew from the east, damaging my ships and driving us here. We humbly ask that you give us fair winds so that we may return home."

Aeolus shook his head. "As a gracious host, I gave you fair winds to help you return home. If your men released them thinking it was treasures, then you surely have drawn the wrath of an Olympian, and I will not risk their vengeance by helping you a second time. Now leave us."

"Wise, Aeolus—" Odysseus began before Aeolus raised a hand to cut him off.

"I said leave us."

"Sire, our ships are in need of repair. If we could..."

Aeolus pounded his fist on the table, stood and shouted, "I said leave us!"

With that, Odysseus bowed and left. He could not risk angering the keeper of the winds. When he reached his ships, he turned to his men. "Make ready to sail."

"What course shall we sail, sire," Eurylochus asked.

Remembering Aeolus earlier warning about the dangers of the Southern seas he replied, "North." North into the uncharted waters of the Western seas.

Poseidon was very happy. His plan worked. Now Odysseus was heading North in ships that were barely seaworthy. He would have to stop and make repairs. He turned and spoke to his fellow Olympians.

"Odysseus thinks he's so clever. He'll have to put in for repairs, and his next stop will surely destroy him." Then he laughed so loud it shook the ground below.

Athena was worried. She knew where Odysseus's course would take him. There was only one thing she could think of to help him, but she had to be careful. If someone found out what she was planning, Poseidon could turn his vengeance against her. She only hoped Odysseus was up to the challenge ahead of him.

CHAPTER 6

THE LAESTRYGONIAN

Seven days passed since leaving Aeolia when the Greeks came across a mysterious island. Odysseus's men were exhausted, and his ships were in desperate need of repairs. They were also running short of supplies. They found a small lagoon surrounded by hills. There was a narrow entrance where his ships could enter. It would serve as a natural harbor to protect them from the sea while repairing their ships. Odysseus signaled his ships to enter. One by one, they entered. When it was time for Odysseus's ship to enter, he received a message from inside the lagoon.

"Sire," Polites said, "we've received word from the ships in the lagoon. There's not enough room for our ship to enter."

Odysseus sighed. His ship needed repairs as well, but he had to look after his men first. He spied a small group of smooth rocks outside the lagoon beside its entrance. There was just enough room to fit a ship between the rocks and the hills around the lagoon. Its location would also let them see inside the lagoon.

"Tie our ship to those rocks," he ordered. "They will provide some protection from the sea. Use wood debris from the storms as bumpers to keep us from rubbing up against them. When the first ship has finished their repairs, we will trade places and begin our repairs."

After his ship was tied to the rocks, Odysseus climbed one of the lagoon's hills to observe the area. Inside the lagoon were eleven of his ships. They were lashed together for better protection. He could see his men starting to make repairs. Outside the lagoon, his ship was nestled between some rocks and the hills surrounding the lagoon, safe for the time being. Beyond the hills surrounding the lagoon were tall trees. He looked around as far as the eye could see and found no paths or any other civilization. Then off in the distance he saw smoke. *Someone must live here*, he thought. He wanted to investigate himself, but his men needed him here.

He returned to his ship. "Eurylochus, Polites," Odysseus said, "tomorrow morning take an aide and go investigate the smoke I saw in the distance. Someone must live here. Find out who they are. I need to stay here and oversee the repairs."

The next morning, the trio climbed the hill and started making their way toward the smoke in the distance. Not long after entering the tree line, they found a path leading toward the smoke and started following it. After about an hour, they came across a young girl in plain cloths carrying a water jar. Even though she was a young girl, she was a full head taller than any of them.

"Who are you?" Eurylochus asked. "What island is this, and who lives here?"

"This land is called Lamos," the girl replied. She pointed to the smoke. "The city off in the distance is Telepylus. I am the daughter of Antiphates, King of the Laestrygonian. I'm on my way to the Fountain of Artakia to fetch some water. This path will take you to my father. He will be happy to meet you."

Eurylochus nodded and signaled the group to move on. "Shouldn't we ask her more about these Laestrygonian?" Polites asked.

"What more could she tell us," Eurylochus answered smugly. "Besides, how dangerous could a people be when their King has to have his daughter fetch his water."

"To begin with, did you notice how large she was?" Polites replied. "A young girl like that and she's taller than any of us. That's not right."

Eurylochus ignored him. Polites said nothing more as they continued on. After another hour, they came across a house larger than any they had ever seen. Two large doors and one man-sized door were in the front.

"These must be city walls," Eurylochus said.

"If these are city walls, then where are the guards?" Polites asked nervously.

They entered the smaller door. The inside was not like any walled city they had seen. It looked more like a house. As they rounded a corner, they found a large woman, twice as large as the dreaded cyclops they faced. Except for her size, she appeared as a normal woman dressed in the same plain cloths as the girl they met earlier. The woman turned and saw them. They trembled with fear as she began to speak.

"Visitors," she said in a polite voice. "It's been a long time since we've had visitors. My husband, King Antiphates, is at an assembly meeting. He will be happy to meet you." Then she turned and called her husband.

The ground shook as her husband approached. When he appeared, they saw he was even larger than his wife. He looked at the trio. Except for his size, he also appeared as a normal man until he smiled. When he smiled, they could see that his mouth was filled with sharp pointed teeth. It was a horrid, wicked smile that it sent cold shivers of terror down their spine. "Welcome to Telepylus," he said with a gracious bow. "I am King Antiphates of the Laestrygonian, and I'm happy to meet you."

Before they reacted, Antiphates reached out, grabbed the aide and began to devour him. Then his wife smiled the same horrid, wicked smile as her husband, showing her sharp pointed teeth. "Yes," she said as her husband continued devouring their companion. "We are all happy to meet you."

"RUN!" Eurylochus shouted. He and Polites ran out of the door and down the path toward the ships. As they ran, they passed the young girl they met earlier. When they looked at her, they could see she gave them the same horrid, wicked smile as her parents. Her mouth was also filled with sharp pointed teeth. "I told you my father would be happy to meet you," she said as they ran past. "It's been a long time since we've *enjoyed* guests such as you."

Eurylochus's legs felt like lead as he raced for the lagoon. Terror filled his heart. If they didn't reach the ships in time, everyone including himself would die. "Keep running, Polites," he cried. We have to make it back to warn the others!"

Polites's legs were rubbery from his fear, but he wasn't about to stop. "With the help of the

Olympians, we'll make it back in time to warn our king!"

Warn our king. Eurylochus almost laughed at that thought. *This island isn't a sanctuary. It's a death trap.* He remembered the cave with the cyclops and the fear and hopelessness he felt as he watched six men eaten by the monster. Now their king had brought them to an island filled with giant cannibals, creatures even larger and deadlier than Polyphemus. *Odysseus is a fool!* he thought. *The sooner we're rid of him the better.*

King Antiphates was busy as well. After finishing his gruesome meal, he began gathering the men of the town. They had work to do.

When Eurylochus and Polites reached the lagoon, they climbed down the hill and boarded their ship. Although winded from their run, Eurylochus managed to speak. "Sire! We must leave now! This island is filled with giant cannibals!" Then he told them what happened.

Before Odysseus could reply, the hills around the lagoon began to shake. Waves threatened to dash their ships on the rocks. As he looked up, he could see that hundreds of giants had climbed to the top of the hills surrounding the lagoon. When the last one reached the top, they began throwing huge boulders at the ships inside.

As Odysseus and his men peered through the entrance, they could see the chaos inside. Men were running across their decks as the boulders crushed them. Ships were snapped in half as if they were twigs. Dead bodies were floating everywhere while the survivors struggled in the water beside them. The screams from their comrades were deafening. Odysseus and his men were certain they were next.

Then Odysseus noticed something. The giants were looking inward toward the lagoon. They had not been seen. "Eurylochus, send the men to their oars and cut the lines. We're getting out of here."

"What about the men in the lagoon?" Eurylochus asked.

Odysseus closed his eyes and shook his head. "There's nothing we can do for them. We can only save ourselves."

As they pulled away from the rocks, the assault from the hills stopped. As they looked inside the entrance, they could see all the ships were gone. The lagoon was filled with wreckage and men. For the dead, their ordeal was over, but for the survivors it had just begun. Several giants entered the lagoon carrying sharpened poles in their hands and baskets at their sides. They began to spear Odysseus's men as if they were fish. One, two, sometimes three men were speared at a time before being placed in a giant's basket to be devoured later at their gruesome evening feast. Each time a man was speared, the giants on the hills cheered. The lagoon's waters turned red with blood. The dead were silent, but the screams of the living as they writhed on the poles tore at their hearts.

"THERE EVERYWHERE!" "SOMEONE HELP ME!" "LOOK OUT, THERE'S ONE BEHIND YOU!" "NO!" "STAY AWAY!" "DON'T LEAVE US" "COME BACK, COME BACK!" The cries of their doomed comrades rang in their ears and tore at their hearts as Odysseus and his men silently rowed away. Their spirts sank at the loss of so many men who had shared their breakfast with them this morning.

Poseidon's rage was uncontrollable. "It should have worked!" he screamed. "It should have worked! The plan was perfect! How did Odysseus survive! The Laestrygonians should have destroyed them all! He should be dead!"

Great earthquakes shook the land and the seas boiled as Athena's uncle vented his rage. It was so bad that Gaia was about call on Zeus to end this madness. Now was the time for her to act.

"Uncle, you must control your anger," she said. "Your rage is justified but if you continue, Gaia may call on Zeus, and he may end your vendetta against Odysseus."

Poseidon calmed himself. "You are right, Athena. Now we know why you are the Olympian of wisdom." He headed off to consider his next plan.

Athena smiled because she knew something Poseidon didn't—he just made his first serious misstep. If an Olympian had a vendetta against a mortal, the others weren't likely to get involved. An Olympian could do almost anything to a mortal—kill or maim them, drown or crush them. They could even feed them to the Hydra. But using cannibals to punish a mortal was never condoned. Not even her sadistic brother Ares would do such a thing. Poseidon's temper was always a source of friction with the other Olympians, but now they were starting to whisper about his use of cannibals, and they didn't like it.

But one misstep wouldn't turn them against Poseidon. Athena looked at Odysseus`s course and realized the new danger he would soon face. She had to help him, but how? If she interfered directly, she would face Poseidon's wrath and her father's punishment. Luckily no one knew what she did at Lamos before Odysseus arrived, but she couldn't risk helping him at his next stop. There had to be a way. There had to be someone who could help, but who?

Then it came to her. She rushed off to find the one Olympian who could help.

CHAPTER 7

CIRCE

Their hearts were filled with grief as Lamos disappeared over the horizon. None of them had experienced the kind of loss they suffered at the hands of the Laestrygonian. When Odysseus left for Troy, he had twelve ships and six hundred men. After ten years of war, he hadn't lost a single man or ship. Now, three months after leaving Troy, there was only one ship and thirty-six men left. There ship seemed like the barge of the dead as they tried to understand and come to terms with the loss, terror, and horror they had just experienced. All of their hearts grieved at the loss they suffered.

Odysseus's sorrow and grief felt like a heavy weight on his heart. He was their king. They trusted him to take them home safely. Now they were dead, and they died a most horrible death. How could he have been so wrong? How could he have made such mistakes? He was only human, but that didn't help relieve the pain. The burdens of leadership could be crushing at times, especially when you were wrong and others suffered because of your mistakes. Right now, he felt as if a mountain was on his chest.

Their ship was barely seaworthy and in desperate need of repairs. They had lost their mast and sail, the deck boards were torn apart, and the sides were cracked and leaking. Under normal conditions, Odysseus wouldn't let anyone sail in their ship, but they had no choice. If they didn't sail, they died. It was that simple.

For two days, they sailed in the uncharted Western Sea before they spotted an island. With the ship needing major repairs, Odysseus ordered them to make landfall on a beach in front of a thick forest. After what happened with the cyclops and Laestrygonians, Odysseus had his men remain on the ship ready to leave in case of danger. On the third day, he left to scout the island. He killed a stag and brought it back to his men so they would have fresh meat. This raised their spirits.

After their meal, he addressed his men. "Men, I know we've been through a lot, but remember Aeolus—he gave us hospitality and tried to help us. We need to divide up in two groups. One group will start repairs on the ship while the other scouts the island to see who lives here. I'll lead the group to scout the island. Eurylochus will remain here and begin repairs on the ship."

"Sire," Eurylochus said, "if we are to return home, the ship needs serious repairs. You are the better shipwright. You need to stay with the ships and get was much done as we can in case there's trouble."

Odysseus thought about what Eurylochus said. He wanted to go with the scouts in case there was trouble, but what Eurylochus said made sense. "We'll draw straws to see who goes with the scouting party." Eurylochus won.

Eurylochus left the boat with twenty-two men. They no longer trusted their surroundings after the brutal deaths they had witnessed. Their feet felt like lead weights dragging at the end of their legs, weary from the war and the tragedies behind them and hesitant to try to move forward.

"Look, men, a forest," Eurylochus called out as he pointed to what others might see as a safe haven—a place of beauty. He paused, though, knowing that dangers lurked in many places he had never suspected. He looked at his men and read the fear in their eyes. He knew he had to try to motivate them if he wanted to both survive this journey and be their leader one day. "There's a good chance some food and supplies are ahead. We are strong and can do this together."

"The men we lost were strong," someone replied.

Eurylochus had no answer. He found a path leading away from the beach. "OK, everyone, we're going to follow this path and see where it takes us." Before long, they saw a beautiful stone house in the distance. Various animals surrounded the house including mountain wolves and lions, dangerous animals that for some reason were very docile and left them alone.

"I don't like this," Eurylochus told the group. "Stay on guard. Anything can happen."

As they approached the gates of the stone house, they looked inside and saw a beautiful woman singing the most beautiful songs. As she worked her loom, they saw that she created a web so fine and soft with such dazzling colors that it rivaled the Olympians.

"Who are you, and what place is this?" Polites called to her.

She stopped her work and looked at them. "I am Circe, and this is the island of Aeaea." The gates slowly opened. "Come in, weary travelers, and enjoy my hospitality."

Polites lead the men into the house. "Wait," Eurylochus said. "Something is not right. I suspect at trap." But the men were too tired and exhausted from their ordeal to listen to him. They entered the house.

Once inside, Circe gave them cheese, honey, meal, and Pramnian wine. Outside, Eurylochus noticed that the men were in a dream like state, completely mesmerized by her charms. As they were enjoying themselves, Eurylochus saw Circe reach under a cloth and pull out a wand. Then she raised it and waved it in the air.

Suddenly the men began to change. Their bodies fattened as arms and legs turned into the legs of an animal. Their hands and feet transformed into what looked like hoofs. Their heads and faces became rounded while their noses became snout like. Eurylochus watched in horror, as all the men who entered the house were turned into swine.

Realizing there was nothing he could do for then, Eurylochus ran back to the ships to warn the others. When he reached the ships, he searched for Odysseus. "Sire!" he cried. "We must leave! This island is cursed by a sorceress!" He proceeded to tell Odysseus what happened.

Odysseus thought the situation over. He'd lost too many men and had no intention of losing any more without a fight. "Take me to her house, Eurylochus."

Overcome with fear, Eurylochus replied, "I cannot, sire. If I do, I'll be turned into a swine.

Please do not go there, sire. For if you do, you will be turned into a swine as well."

Realizing Eurylochus was unable to proceed due to his fear, Odysseus had him point the way to the house. He grabbed his sword and arrows and began making his way there. On the way, he heard a voice he never heard before. "I can't believe one of my descendants is foolish enough to try and use brute force to defeat a sorceress instead of using the gifts I've given him." Odysseus looked up and saw a young man approaching him from above. When the man got closer, he saw the winged sandals on his feet and a caduceus in his hands. Was this his great grandfather, the Olympian Hermes?

Normally, Hermes would not have wasted his time on such a distant relation, but his sister Athena approached him asking for his help. Hermes was close to Athena not because they were siblings but because they valued cunning and trickery above all other traits. He knew Athena watched after Odysseus and his family, so when she came to him for help, he agreed. If it aggravated their uncle, Poseidon, well that was a bonus.

"You really think your sword and arrows are going to do anything against Circe?" Hermes chided Odysseus. "You won't get within arrow shot before she dispatches you. Turn around and leave this place, save yourself."

Odysseus dropped to bended knee. This was his chance to enlist the aid of an Olympian to help him free his men. "Great Hermes, messenger of the great and powerful Zeus, I have lost too many men on this journey and cannot stand by and lose any more. This Circe may be a sorceress, but you are greater. I will do all in my power to slay her and free my men from her spell. Honor, courage, and the will of the Olympians will help me carry the day."

Hermes leaned in and scowled at Odysseus. "Stop trying to trick a trickster, Odysseus. It's not going to work. If you try it again, the next Olympian you'll see will be Hades!" Then he pulled back, smiled, shrugged, and continued in a jovial tone. "Of course, I would have been disappointed if you hadn't tried."

Then Hermes's voice turned serious. "Honor and courage will not help you today, Odysseus. Only your greatest gifts, cunning and trickery, will save you and your men. Circe is a powerful sorceress and an immortal, so you cannot kill her. She likes to use powerful potions to put men in a stupor, and then she strikes. This is what she did before she turned your men into swine."

Then he leaned over and dug up a strange root. "This is Moly. Only Olympians can uproot it, so don't waste it. It will protect you from the potions Circe puts in the food and wine." He handed it to Odysseus who ate it. "When she offers you food and drink, you must accept. She will become confused when her potions do not affect you." Hermes paused for a moment. "But you must be vigilant and wary, Odysseus, for some time during your encounter, she will reach for her wand. That's the time to act."

"Even though Circe is also immortal, she can be maimed, and she knows this. When she reaches for her wand, you must draw your sword and threaten her—threaten her as if you were a madman. You must convince her that your anger is such that you will cause such an injury that it will never heal. If she doesn't believe you, she will simply strike you down."

"If you convince her of this, she will become afraid and will not be able to use her magic. She will then start to desire you and wish to take you to her bed. You must not refuse, but do not be taken by her beauty and charm. Before you go with her, you must make her promise to do no harm to you. As an immortal, if she ever breaks a promise, she will be rendered senseless and lose her powers and immortality. She knows this as well. If you go with her before you get her promise, she will kill you, and that will be the end of you and your men."

With that the Hermes left. Odysseus rose and continued on. Before long, he reached the stone house and knocked at the gate. He noticed a large herd of swine in a pen beside the house.

A beautiful woman appeared. "Hello, weary stranger. My name is Circe. Please come in and enjoy my hospitality."

"Thank you, fair maiden," Odysseus said as he bowed. Then he entered the house. It was large and ornate.

"What is your name, traveler?"

"Odysseus"

Circe led him to some comfortable pillows on the floor. "Come, Odysseus, enjoy some wine, cheese, and honey."

Odysseus nodded and began to enjoy the delicacies. "Are there others on this island?" he asked.

"I have attendants, but no, there is no one else. Just me."

Odysseus nodded. "How long have you lived here and how did you come across such wonderful food and drink?" he asked as he enjoyed some cheese.

"I've lived here for some time. As far as the food and drink, I manage with my attendants."

Odysseus drank some wine. "We saw no ships or harbor. Are you shipwrecked? Do you need passage?"

Circe offered him some honey. "No, thank you. I can manage on my own."

Her answers were cryptic. *Good*, Odysseus thought. *That's what I want.* "Have there been any other travelers passing by?"

"Some," she said. As their conversation continued, Odysseus continued to eat and drink the offerings Circe gave him. He also noticed how confused she appeared.

When she thought his back was turned, Circe made her way over to a stand. Ten years of war with the Trojans had sharpened his eyes more than she realized. She put her hand under a cloth and brought out her wand.

"YOU EVIL WITCH!" Odysseus screamed. Witch was not a word sorceresses liked. Only a madman would use such a term, which is what he was counting on. He drew his sword, lunged at her, and pushed her to the floor. "I'll gouge out your eyes, cut off your arms, and feed them to your hogs for trying to cast a spell on me!"

Circe was taken aback. "How dare you accuse me of sorcery. I am but a simple ..."

"Silence witch!" Odysseus yelled, cutting her off. "You live here alone, no cities or town. There are no workers, yet there is plenty of food and wine. No ships or harbor yet you're able to leave this island whenever you want. Only a witch can do such work. And my men. I sent twenty-two up here this morning and only one came back. Now you have twenty-one swine in your pen. You've cast your last spell, witch!"

Odysseus raised his sword and started to bring it down. "No!" she yelled. Odysseus could see the terror in her eyes as he held his hand. Those same eyes gave way to desire. Then she gave him a seductive smile. "You must be weary from your travels. Come with to my private chambers, and I will help you relax from your travels."

"Only if you promise by the Olympians not to harm me or my men and to restore my men to human form before sunset and aid us in our journey."

"Wouldn't you like to visit my private chambers first and ..."

"PROMISE!" Odysseus yelled with a wild look in his eyes.

Circe realized she was up against a strong-willed individual. He was going to tear her apart if he had the chance. Eventually, she would kill him but little comfort that would be if he gouged out her eyes or cut her arms off. She had to give in. "I promise by the Olympians to do what you ask."

Odysseus lowered his sword and retired with her to her private chambers. Afterwards, just as she promised, Circe went out to the pen outside, waved her wand, and returned his men to human form.

"There are tools and supplies in a shed that you can use to repair you ship," Circe said. "You and your men can expect my true hospitality as well."

Odysseus gave her a concerned look.

"Fear not, Odysseus. I have promised by the Olympians to do no harm to you or your men and aid you on your journey. I will keep my promise."

"Thank you, Circe," he said. "I will take my men down to the beach and reassure those who are with the ship. Then I will return for the supplies to repair our vessel as well as for food and drink to fortify my men."

At the beach, Eurylochus was considering leaving because he did not believe Odysseus would succeed. *He has led us to disaster,* he thought. *Perhaps I should be in charge instead of Odysseus.* He was thinking those thoughts when someone yelled, "There they are!" Everyone looked up and saw Odysseus returning with their shipmates.

"We have nothing more to fear from Circe," Odysseus began. "She has promised by the Olympians not to harm us and help us on our journey. We have access to tools to repair our ship and fine foods to replenish our bodies. We will also have time to rest and invigorate our spirits."

"No, sire." It was Eurylochus. "We must leave this accursed island at once. Circe is evil and will do us harm. Do not trust her."

"She has promised by the Olympians. She cannot break her word without experiencing their wrath."

Eurylochus wasn't swayed. "You led us to the island of the cyclops, and we lost six men. The Laestrygonian destroyed all but one of our ships and killed or remaining comrades. We are lost in the uncharted Western Sea, in a wrecked ship on an island with a sorceress, one who has already tried to do harm us. No, sire, do not lead us into more misfortune by staying here. Leave now while we can."

Being challenged by his second-in-command, bringing up of their misfortune, and reminding him of the mistakes he made was more than the exhausted Odysseus could stand. He lunged at Eurylochus. He would have killed him if his men hadn't pulled them apart. "We cannot leave until we have repaired our ship and replenished our bodies," Odysseus told his men. "Only then can we face the challenges of the Western Sea. For now, it's time to work." As his men started working on their ship, Odysseus leaned in to Eurylochus and whispered, "Be thankful you're my sister's husband."

As time went on, the Greeks repaired their ship and replenished their bodies. One day Odysseus was standing atop a hill overseeing the work when Circe came up from behind. "Your men are skilled workers," she said. "They will repair your ship although it will take a long time to do so."

Odysseus and his men had come to terms with Circe. She didn't harm them as she promised, and they behaved themselves. She was a sorceress after all. "They only desire to return home. They will repair the ship, and then we will leave." Then he looked at her. "What can you tell me about the Western Sea and the best way to get home."

"Unfortunately, I cannot tell you anything, but there is someone who can—the blind Theban clairvoyant Teiresias."

A shocked look appeared on Odysseus`s face. "He's dead."

Circe slowly turned and gave him a concerned look. "Yes, Odysseus. In order to return home, you must journey to the land of the dead and speak with Teiresias. He is the only one who can give you a path home, tell you the trials you must face, and why your journey is fraught with such peril. I can help you go and return safely, but I cannot go with you. That is the only way you can return home."

Odysseus would have suspected treachery but for her promise. *I must travel to the land of the dead in order to return home.* Neither one said a word as they watched his men continue working on their ship.

Hermes and Athena were on Mount Olympus as their uncle raged in the other room.

"Hermes, you will suffer for this!" Poseidon yelled. His temper shook the Earth below.

"He's furious with you," Athena told her younger brother.

Hermes shrugged. "Not much he can do about it. Father isn't interested in an Olympian's vendetta with a mortal, and Odysseus is my great grandson. I have a claim, no matter how small, to help him. In addition, as the messenger of the Olympians and father's personal herald, I can't be out of service for too long. Father will give me some small punishment to save face, but it will be nothing compared to what he would have done to another Olympian such as ..."

Hermes paused at what he was about to say. Then he smiled, chuckled, and looked at Athena. "Well played sister, well played."

Athena gave him a sly smile. "What do you mean?" she said acting as innocent as she could.

"Oh, don't act so innocent with me," Hermes said with a laugh. "You wanted to help Odysseus, but if you or any other Olympian interfered with Poseidon's vendetta, you would face severe punishment from father. Since he's my great grandson, I could claim a right to help him. You knew I'd only get a slap on the wrist, so why not have me do your work for you. Well done indeed."

Athena's smile grew larger as she realized her little brother figured it out. Then Hermes put his arms around her shoulder.

"Congratulations, big sis," he said with a smile. "You just tricked a trickster."

CHAPTER 8

LAND OF THE DEAD

I t's time, sire."

Odysseus turned to see Polites standing behind him. They had been on Circe's island for the past year repairing their ship and rejuvenating their bodies. Now they were ready to go. In addition, Odysseus made amends with Eurylochus. He wasn't in a hurry to leave because he knew what they had to do next. He was also enjoying the pleasures of Circe which concerned his men. That was probably the reason why Polites came to talk to him. The others wouldn't dare such a thing.

"OK, Polites," he said, "assemble the men. I'll be along soon and will address them when I get there."

After Polites left, Circe came up to him and handed him something. "Here, you'll need this."

Odysseus looked at the object. It was a wooden sword. "Why do I need this?"

"The spirits don't fear normal weapons," she said. But this sword has been bathed in the river Styx. If it touches them, it will burn like the fires of Tartarus. It's the only thing that will keep them at bay." She continued. "Do you remember everything I told you?"

Odysseus nodded and reviewed their plan.

"What about the man who died last night?" she asked.

Odysseus closed his eyes and winced. Last night Elpenor, the youngest member of their group, died when he got drunk and fell off the roof of Circe's house. They had to leave now because the conditions were right for their journey to the underworld, so they didn't have time to give him a proper burial. "We've done all we can. If we don't leave now, we'll be delayed another six months." Then he turned to her. "It's time for us to leave."

This was painful for Circe. She had fallen in love with him, but because of her promise not to harm him or his men and aid them in their journey, she could do nothing. "Safe journey, Odysseus, to you and your men," was all she said. Then she turned and walked away.

Odysseus made his way down to the beach. Their ship looked like it just came out of the shipyard. They had a new mast and sail. The deck boards had been replaced, and the leaks had been fixed. It was loaded with supplies, and they were ready to go. His men were gathered around waiting to hear what he had to say.

"Men, it's time for us to return home to our loved ones," he began, "but before we do, we must find a way out of the Western Sea, and there is only one who we can ask to find our way home—the clairvoyant Teiresias." There was mumbling amongst his men. "Yes, that means a trip to the underworld, but Circe has given us a way to go there and return without harm to ourselves." He explained their plan to them. The men accepted this as a matter of course. A year ago, this would never have happened, but their spirits had healed as they repaired their ship. "Then make sail. It's time to go home."

His men loaded onto their ship and raised their sail. From the beach, Circe raised her wand. A fair wind started to blow, a wind that would take them to the underworld.

A day out, their lookout cried, "Grey mist ahead."

Odysseus looked ahead. A large gray mist as far as the eye could see appeared in front of them, the path to the underworld. Circe had conjured the mist to take them to the end of the world, far beyond Oceanus to the land of the Cimmerians. If they turned away, it would disappear. If they held their course, they would begin their journey. "Straight ahead," he ordered as their ship entered the mist.

Inside was a land permanently deprived of sunlight, a land shrouded in mist and darkness. This was the realm of Hades. A place Circe warned them about: "Time inside has stopped while the rest of the world continues on. So don't delay or all that you love will have turned to dust before you return."

A cold shiver ran down Odysseus's spine as they approached the shore. Even after everything they've been through, this place terrified him like no other. While he feared the living and immortals, he knew he could handle anything that was alive. If it was living, it could be killed. If it were immortal, it could be fooled. But this place—this place would petrify the stoutest heart of the bravest warrior. The spirts could not be handled like regular men, and if he wasn't careful he would surely join them.

Odysseus looked at his men. Even though they were rested and rejuvenated after their stay on Circe's island, he could tell that every one of them felt as he did. "Be strong men," he said in a reassuring voice. "After we meet with Teiresias, we will be on our way."

While everyone understood this was necessary to return home, all of them feared what could happen—a fear justified by the trials they faced and men they lost.

Soon they reached a rocky beach in front of a large cave. Odysseus gathered a group of men and walked toward the cave. As they approached it, they saw a dark shadow marking one of the entrances to the underworld. Circe warned them not to step across into the cave. If they did, they would join the spirits.

Odysseus looked at Perimedes, a friend of his. "Let's go. We have work to do."

Using special tools, they dug a hole one cubit by one cubit just inside of the shadowed area of the cave without stepping across its boundary. Then they filled it with honey, milk, wine, and water, sprinkled with white barley meal and ram's blood, a delicacy for the spirits.

As Circe predicted, many spirits approached. "You must keep them away or they will finish the meal before Teiresias appears, then all will be lost," she had warned him. They ignored his men's spears and swords as she said they would but when Odysseus drew the wooden sword that had been bathed in the river Styx, they retreated.

The first spirit to approach was that of Elpenor. Odysseus allowed him to approach. After he ate, he began to speak. "Odysseus, why did you not give me a proper burial?"

Odysseus was taken aback by the question. "Our time was short, and we needed to sail or all hope would be lost. Conditions would no longer be right for us to reach the underworld. We did not have time to perform the burial rights."

"You must return and give me a proper burial or all the Olympians will be against you, and you will never return home."

Odysseus was concerned. This was not part of their plan, but he did not want to incur the wrath of the Olympians. "We will return and give you a proper burial, Elpenor."

With that, Elpenor left. It was some time before the next spirit arrived. It was walking slowly as it approached the pit. Its form was that of an old man. Everyone realized who it was—the blind Theban clairvoyant Teiresias.

Odysseus allowed him to approach. As he ate his meal, he began to speak. "I know what you want from me, Odysseus, but before I help you, I must tell something. You insulted a powerful Olympian. That is the reason you and your men are lost, wandering, and suffering."

This surprised Odysseus. He did everything he could to stay on the Olympians' good side. What could he have done to insult one of them? "I have done nothing to offend anyone least of all the Olympians. I have defended myself in times of danger. What have I done to insult them?"

"Polyphemus, the cyclops you encountered, is the son of Poseidon. When you blinded Polyphemus, you stirred Poseidon's anger, and now he seeks revenge. Then you mocked and insulted Poseidon when Polyphemus called for his father's vengeance against you, angering him further and costing you the support of the other Olympians. You still would have escaped Poseidon's wrath if you had not foolishly given Polyphemus your real name. That`s how Poseidon knows who you are. Odysseus, your pride and arrogance is the reason why you and your men are suffering."

It took a moment for this to sink in. All this could have been avoided if he had controlled himself when they escaped the cyclops. He wanted the rest of the beasts to know of his deed, but he never expected to anger an Olympian. Pride and arrogance, the twin sins that have undone many a man, had cost him a swift return home. He had to remember to control both in the future.

Then he turned to Teiresias. "What must we do to return home?"

Teiresias spoke. "You will have to stay in the Western Sea. If you enter the Southern Sea, Poseidon will find you, and you will never return home. First you must return to Aeaea and give Elpenor a proper burial. When you leave, head north until you reach the continent, then travel east keeping close to the land. Poseidon will not be able to find you if stay close to the land. That's Zeus`s domain. But you will face two trials on this path—first Sirens then Charybdis and Scylla."

"Who are the Sirens, Charybdis, and Scylla?" Odysseus asked.

"Two dangers that will destroy you if you do not find a way past them because if you travel out into the sea, Poseidon will surely find you," was all Teiresias would say. Then he continued.

"After these trials, you will enter the Eastern Sea and come to the island of Thrinacian, the home of the cattle of Helios, an immortal and keeper of the sun. Under no circumstance should you land on Thrinacian because anyone who harms the cattle of Helios will pay with their lives. When you see the island, set a course east. You will be home before Poseidon can find you. Then you make peace with the Olympian."

With that, Teiresias ate his fill and left. Odysseus was surprised to see the spirit that arrived next. It was his mother Anticlea.

"Mother!" he cried. He was about to step across the boundary when his mother raised her hand to stop him.

"My son, it's good to see you."

"What happened?"

"I died of grief waiting for you," she said, "but do not dwell on that. There is trouble at home. Usurpers, one hundred and eight of them, are trying to steal your throne. They believe you are dead and are trying to force your wife, Penelope, to marry one of them. Fear not, she knows you are alive and has been loyal and true to you, but you must hurry home to save everyone." Then his mother ate her fill and left.

The spirit of Agamemnon arrived next. Odysseus was shocked to see the leader of the Greek forces. "Oh, great Agamemnon, I am saddened to see you here. Your ship must have sunk on the return voyage."

Agamemnon shook his head. "No, Odysseus, I did arrive home safely, but my homecoming was a tragic one. I was killed by my wife and her lover. She was angry at me for my having to sacrifice our daughter before we could set sail for our war against Troy. She took a lover, waited for my return, and then murdered me. Now my son seeks revenge on my wife and her lover. He plans on killing them both when he is older. If he does, the Olympians will punish him. They will unleash the Furies on him, and his life will be one of torment and agony. My house is turmoil, brave Odysseus, and it pains me even in the underworld."

He paused before continuing. "But fear not, Odysseus, because your wife is loyal and true to you. She knows you're alive and awaits your return. However, when you return, do not burden her with everything that happened to you. Only tell her part of the tale. You have been gone for a long time, and it will cause her great pain and anguish to know how dreaded your voyage has been. Do not distress her. Keep your marriage a loving and happy one." Then he ate his fill and left.

The spirit of Achilles arrived next. Odysseus was shocked to see him. "Achilles, you are the greatest warrior of us all. Men will sing of your deeds for ages! How you slew Hector and stopped the Trojans from reaching our ships. How you vanquished the Amazon queen Penthesilea and her female warriors. The Trojan allies you conquered and foes you defeated. Without you, we would have surely failed. No one will ever forget the deeds..."

Achilles raised his hand to cut him off. "I would rather be a live farmer than a dead hero," he said. "Great deeds count for nothing when compared to the joys of caressing your wife or holding your children. The joy you feel when your child laughs for the first time or seeing them take their first step. I would trade all those valiant deeds in and become servant in a poor man's house if I could experience the real joys in life. The greatest warrior among the dead is nothing to being a simple man among the living. Remember this, Odysseus, when you return home." Then he ate his fill and left.

Others came—Tyro, Antiope, Epicaste, Leda, Iphimedeia, Phaedra, Procris, the fair Ariadne, Maera, Clymene, and Eriphyle. More came as well to speak with Odysseus. Soon the mixture was gone, and it was time to leave.

"Let's go, men," Odysseus said. They loaded their ship and reversed course. As they started to leave, a fair wind arose to blow them out of the land of the Cimmerians, just as Circe told them would happen. Soon they were out of the dark mist and in clear skies. They looked behind them, and the dark mist they entered was gone."

A day later, they arrived at Aeaea where a puzzled Circe was waiting on the beach. "Why have you returned?" she asked Odysseus.

"We returned to give Elpenor a proper burial. We will be leaving in the morning." Then he returned the wooden sword to her. That evening after the burial ceremony, Circe approached Odysseus and asked him about his journey to the underworld. He told her what Teiresias said. "Do you know anything about these trials?" he asked.

Circe nodded. "The Sirens will be the first trial you will face. They are three creatures—part woman, part bird—that live on the island of Sirenum Scopuli, a few days sailing from here. Their songs are so beautiful that any man who hears it will become enchanted and try to swim to them. The rocks surrounding their island prevent anyone from reaching the shore, so those unlucky enough to hear them will drown. The currents around their island are strong, so keep your men at their oars or your ship will be wrecked on the rocks. If you try to avoid them, you will sail too far out to sea, and Poseidon will find you. The only way to avoid their songs is to put beeswax in your ears until you pass them by. Some men have tried to hear their sweet songs and not join them by having their crews tie them to their ship masts until they pass, but I do not recommend it. These men always become enchanted, find a way to free themselves, and drown trying to reach the Sirens."

"Charybdis and Scylla will be your next trial. A few days past the Sirens, you will come to a large island close to the continent. You must pass between them. Both sides of the passageway have high cliffs, so you won't be able to beach your ship, and the current is so strong that once you enter you will not be able to stop until you exit. The end of the passageway narrows so that each side is within bow shot of each other. That's where you'll find Charybdis and Scylla."

"On one side is Charybdis. She is one of Poseidon's daughters who sided with him against Zeus during her father's revolt and sank several of his islands. Zeus punished her by turning her into a giant creature with an unquenchable thirst for sea water. She drinks so much sea water that she creates a whirlpool that sucks everything down: ships, fish, men, everything. After her thirst is quenched, she stops drinking and the whirlpool ends. She then spits out the debris and digests the living. Her thirst quickly returns, and she starts drinking again, causing the whirlpool to form again. Three times a day she does this. Zeus chained her to the sea floor, and she cannot move. A large fig tree that always blooms is growing on top of a tall cliff. This marks her position for all who pass by."

"On the opposite side is Scylla, a hideous creature with twelve feet, dog heads around her waist, and six large necks. At the end of each neck is a mouth that has three rows of razor-sharp teeth. She lives across from Charybdis on a cliff so high it cannot be reached with an arrow shot. Her six mouths snatch anything that tries to pass: fish, dolphins, and sailors."

"You must choose between the two. If you choose Charybdis, you will lose your ship and all your men. If you choose Scylla, you will lose some of your men but not all them. After Scylla strikes, cry out to her mother, Crataeis, not to let Scylla strike again. If she decides to help you, only six will perish."

Odysseus thought for a moment. "If it`s an island, why can't I sail around the other side?"

"You'll never make it past the wondering rocks on the south side of the island—rocks so smooth and tall that no man can climb them and seas so violent no ship can pass through them. To avoid them, you will have to travel so far out to sea that Poseidon will find you. All who have tried to pass through them have lost their ships to the rocks and drown. Those who survive and reach the shore are devoured by the one-eyed giants who live on the island."

Odysseus sighed. "Cyclops."

"You've heard of them?" she asked. Odysseus told her the tale. "Well, you don't have to worry about them on the north or west side of the island or in the passageway of Charybdis and Scylla. They never travel there."

Then Circe noticed the tormented look on his face. "It's not an easy decision to make Odysseus, but you must choose. To avoid Charybdis, you must face Scylla. To avoid Scylla, you must face Charybdis." Then she looked at him with a cold, serious look on her face. "I know it's cruel to say this, but it's better to lose six men than all of them."

After a moment, she continued. "Teiresias is correct—you must not land on the island of Thrinacian. Anyone who harms the cattle of Helios will pay for it with their lives. It's not worth the risk, so take your bearing, sail past the island, and return home as fast as you can."

With that, Circe finished. "Thank you, Circe, for everything you have done for me and my men," Odysseus said.

"I will miss you, Odysseus," she replied. "I would offer you and your men eternal youth if you stayed on Aeaea, but I know your hearts belong to your loved ones at home. Safe journeys to you and your men." With that she turned and walked away.

The next morning, Odysseus and his men loaded their ship and sailed north. As they looked back, they saw Circe on the beach. She raised her wand, and a fair breeze filled their sail as it carried them north.

Poseidon was furious. "Where are they!" he thundered. "What has that accursed witch Circe done with them!" Great waves formed as his anger grew.

Athena only smiled. She knew where he was. Her owl of wisdom was tracking his every movement. Odysseus was cunning. Taking the northern route was filled with more danger, but it was the only route where Poseidon couldn't find them. He was looking in the Southern Sea. Even if Poseidon discovered Odysseus was in the Western Sea, he wouldn't go near the coast because he would not risk Zeus's wrath after his attempted rebellion. He'd never admit it, but Athena knew it was the truth. Even more important, every time Odysseus outfoxed Poseidon, his temper would get the better of him and his anger would explode. This cost him the support of the other Olympians.

Now she could only watch as Odysseus faced his next challenge.

CHAPTER 9

THE SIRENS

A few days after leaving Aeaea, the Greeks approached Sirenum Scopuli, home of the Sirens. Odysseus had already plugged most of his men's ears with beeswax, but now he was having two of his men bind him firmly to the mast so that he could hear their songs and not be drawn to them. At dusk, his men would check Odysseus, and if he could not here the Sirens' songs, he would be released.

Eurylochus had other ideas. He had never forgiven Odysseus for attacking him on Circes Island or threatening him. He felt Odysseus was a fool who would get all of them killed. There were only thirty-five of them left, and he was going to make it home alive. Now was his chance to dispose of their king.

Lycaon, Amphialos, and Eurylochus tied their king to the mast. Lycaon and Amphialos had been growing more unstable since their encounter with the cyclops, so he included them in his plot. They would tie their king to the mast but leave just enough slack so that he could undo his binds, dive overboard, and die on the rocks by the Siren's island. Then he would take over and have Lycaon and Amphialos executed for their incompetence.

"Make sure the binds are tight, Eurylochus," Odysseus ordered.

"They are, sire," he replied. When they finished, he had them place beeswax in their ears and then had Lycaon and Amphialos return to their oars. Onward they went. Eurylochus would not be at an oar. He would be one of the men watching the ship.

As they approached the island, Odysseus's head began to swoon as a sweet song filled his ears. His men continued to row as the song grew louder. Odysseus began to tug at his binds. As they came closer to the island, the song became louder. Odysseus longed to be with the Sirens. "Release me!" he cried.

With the beeswax in their ears, his men did not hear the song or their king. They rowed on. The closer they came, the greater the longing in Odysseus's heart. "I am your king!" he cried. "I order you to release me." His men ignored his pleas as he pulled harder at his binds.

From his position in the ship, Eurylochus could view Odysseus while not looking directly at him. He was pulling harder and harder at his binds. Soon they would begin to loosen, and he would escape. Odysseus would dive overboard and drown as he tried to reach the Sirens, and then he, Eurylochus, would be in charge. It was only a matter of time.

The songs grew louder in Odysseus's ears, and the longing grew stronger in his heart. "I must be with them! I must! I must!" He pulled and pulled at his binds, but they held him fast. Soon they were close enough to see them—three strange creatures, half female, half bird. It was also where their songs were the strongest. Odysseus screamed in torment as he wrestled with his binds.

Then it happened. He found the gap Eurylochus and his conspirators left. Slowly he began to work his way out of his ropes. Slowly but surely, the binds slackened. He would have freed himself if it had not been for Perimedes. He was not at an oar this day when he noticed Odysseus was about to free himself from the mast.

"Sire!" Perimedos yelled as he ran from the back of the ship to his king and began to tighten his bonds. "You must remain bound, or you will die."

"Unhand me, you swine!" Odysseus yelled at Perimedes. "I must join them! Unhand me, I say!" Even if Perimedes could hear his king, he would not have obeyed him. He continued to tie the binds tighter, but it was just too difficult. Odysseus would eventually make his escape.

Even though they could not hear what was going on, some of the oarsmen saw Perimedes run to the mast and realized something was wrong. They looked at the mast to see their king struggling to get free. They could not leave their oars, but they did alert each other. Each oarsman shook the person next to him and pointed to Odysseus. They recognized their king's danger but could do nothing. If they left their stations, the current would wreck their boat on the rocks. Eventually an oarsman shook Eurylochus on the shoulder.

When Eurylochus looked at the oarsman, he saw him pointing at their struggling king. He also saw the other oarsman looking at him expecting him to do something. This put Eurylochus in a difficult position. His plan was working. Odysseus would eventually free himself and dive overboard to his death, then he would be in charge. But now the oarsmen were alerted to the danger and looking at him to do something. If he did nothing and let Odysseus free himself, they would never trust or follow him. They may even munity. He had no choice. He leapt from his seat, rushed to Odysseus, and helped Perimedes secure his bonds. They struggled for hours rebinding what Odysseus had undone.

Finally, they were far enough away from the Sirens that their songs could no longer be heard by Odysseus. When this happened, Odysseus stopped struggling. At dusk, Eurylochus and Perimedes went forward and looked at their king. He nodded, signaling he could no longer hear their melody. Then Perimedes and Eurylochus released him.

Odysseus removed the beeswax from their ears. "Thank you," he said to both of them. Then he went on to remove the beeswax from the rest of his crew. Eurylochus could only watch as his best chance to do away with his king came to pass.

CHAPTER 10

CHARYBDIS AND SCYLLA

A few days passed before the Greeks spotted the large island Circe told them about and the passageway between it and the continent. The entrance was wide and the current was strong when they entered. High cliffs dominated both sides. There was no going back. Odysseus had not told them everything about the passage. He told his men about Charybdis but not Scylla. Circe was right. It was better to lose six men instead of the entire ship and crew. He did not tell them about Scylla because he feared that if they knew some of them would die, they would veer away and be sucked down by Charybdis. He could only hope that Crataeis would hear his plea and not allow Scylla to strike a second time.

As they continued, the passage grew narrower and narrower. "Look, sharp men," Odysseus told his sailors, "we're coming to the narrowest part." For a moment, he hoped

Charybdis had finished drinking and they could pass over her in safety.

As they drew closer, they began to hear a roaring sound. Then, on the starboard side, he saw a fig tree in full bloom on top of a cliff. *Charybdis*, he thought. The roaring sound grew louder and louder as they approached the narrows. Charybdis was sucking down the water. They could not pass that way.

"Charybdis is drinking in water men," he said. "Stay to the port side and row as hard and as fast as you can so we are not sucked in."

Their ship veered to the port side. As they came closer, they saw the whirlpool Odysseus told them about. It was a huge vortex that drew in all the water from the area. The only water not affected was a narrow current next to the port side cliffs. They steered towards them to avoid being sucked down by Charybdis.

As they entered the narrows, Odysseus looked up. Directly across from the whirlpool was a large cave. *Maybe Scylla's asleep*, he thought. *With all the bad luck we've had so far, a little good luck wouldn't hurt.*

As they came closer, they heard a strange growl like a nearby pack of dogs. "Row faster, men," Odysseus said. "Let's get through this as fast as we can."

The closer they came to the cave, the louder the growling sound became. Then it turned into howling. Odysseus noticed some of his men became concerned. "Stay focused, men," he tried to reassure them. "We're almost through."

They were just below the cave when Scylla appeared. She was as hideous and terrifying as Circe described. She was large with twelve feet and dog heads around her waist. Atop her body were six necks and a grotesque mouth atop each. When she saw the Greeks, the dog heads began barking. Then each mouth gave a streaking cry revealing three rows of razor-sharp teeth. Their cry could terrorize the stoutest heart.

"ROW!" Odysseus screamed.

Scylla approached the edge of the cave and screamed one more time. With blinding speed, all six heads shot downward, grabbing six of Odysseus's men. When her jaws clamped on the helpless victims, blood spattered over everyone and the ship's deck. Then, as quick as she struck, she withdrew her six heads upward and backed into her cave.

Her victims' screams were deafening. "HELP US PLEASE!" "SIRE, DON'T LEAVE US!" "SAVE US!" "PLEASE HELP US!" A sickening crunching sound could be heard from her cave, but there was nothing they could do. The men rowed as fast as they could as Scylla devoured her meal. Their only hope was to row past her before she struck again. As they rowed, the screams became quieter. When they stopped, Scylla appeared a second time, her dog heads barking even louder. Suddenly, her six mouths gave another screeching cry.

The men were horrified because they were still too close! The beast was going to strike again and devour six more of them! They were about to panic when Odysseus stood up in the boat and cried, "Oh great and powerful immortal Crataeis, here our pleas! Please grant us mercy and keep Scylla from striking again!"

As the creature was about to strike, the men noticed that her necks began to sway. The barking from the dog heads lessened, and the mouths no longer shrieked. It was as if the creature was confused or couldn't find them.

"ROW!" Odysseus ordered. "Row with all your strength!" The Greeks rowed with all their strength, moving their ship as fast as they could. When Scylla seemed to recover her senses. She looked at them and screamed but did not strike. They were too far away. Everyone watched as she retreated into her cave. They were safe.

A strange calm came over the ship. Not a word was spoken, but Odysseus knew they were all thinking the same thing. *How did our King know the name of the monster and who to call on for help when she attacked?*

CHAPTER 11

THE CATTLE OF HELIOS

That evening, the mood in the ship was one of shock and bewilderment. They had just lost six men to Scylla including Lycaon, Amphialos, Perimedes, and Polites. The blood of their comrades covered the ship and every man on board. The stench was unbearable. Every man realized that it was only by the grace of the Fates they weren't the one devoured by the monster. The horror from yesterday drained their spirits and poisoned their hearts to the point that they were ready to give up. It seemed like their oars were made of lead as they drove their ship through a sea of tar.

Worst of all, their king seemed to have known what was coming and didn't tell them. *What else wasn't he telling us?* they thought. *Maybe Eurylochus was right, Odysseus wasn't the man for the job. He had been saying as much since they left the cyclops. The Laestrygonian and Circe was something Odysseus couldn't have foreseen, but this? Clearly, he knew what was coming, yet he never warned us.* Distrust of their king slowly began to take hold of the crew.

Odysseus was no more immune to the pain than his men. *Lycaon and Amphialos had lost their senses,* Odysseus thought. *At least they are out of pain.* But the loss of Perimedes and Polites hurt him deeply. Polites was his dearest friend. He had always been there for Odysseus. Perimedes was a good friend who helped him in the land of the dead and saved his life when they passed the Sirens. The pain tore at his heart, and he would miss them dearly.

It was during times like this he wished he wasn't a king. He wished he was just a commoner working the field or an oarsman on a cargo ship. Let someone else carry the burden of leadership. Let someone else make the hard decisions. Let someone else be responsible for the lives of others. All he had to do was follow orders, and if something went wrong and people died, well at least it wasn't his fault. He wouldn't have to live with the guilt.

The next morning, they came across another island. "Sire, do you know anything about this island?" Eurylochus asked.

"It's the island of Thrinacian," Odysseus replied. "Home of the cattle of Helios, the keeper of the sun. If we sail east from here, we will be home in a few days."

"Are there any monsters or dangers here?"

"No monsters, but plenty of danger. We will take a bearing east and head home. We need to avoid this island."

"I have heard of this island, sire," Eurylochus replied. "It is indeed the island that holds the cattle of Helios. It is filled with plenty of clear streams and has fair weather. Helios has removed everything that can harm them so there is no danger."

Odysseus looked at him. "There are plenty of dangers. Anyone who harms one of Helios's cattle will pay for it with their lives."

"Sire, we have plenty of supplies," Eurylochus said. "The only thing we may need is water, and that won't harm the cattle. Sire, let the men land on the island, rest, cook a warm meal, and recover from yesterday's ordeal. The men need this."

Odysseus looked at the men. His men had just been through a terrible ordeal. While they felt the pain of the cyclops and Laestrygonian, this was the first trial that directly affected them. Many still had the blood of their shipmates on them. He was afraid that if he refused their request, they would munity. It was clear that Eurylochus was whispering amongst them again, probably blaming him for all their troubles.

"I will land on the island if every man on this ship promises not to harm the cattle of Helios," he replied. Every man agreed, and the Greeks made landfall.

The Greeks weren't the only ones on the island. Helios's daughters, Lampetia and Phaethusa, were there as well. They tended and guarded the cattle. Phaethusa was on her way to visit their father on Mount Olympus when the Greeks landed. They were worried until they noticed the Greeks stayed on the beach. They collected fresh water from a nearby stream, but that wasn't anything to be concerned about.

"I don't believe these visitors plan on harming father's cattle," Phaethusa told Lampetia.

"I agree," Lampetia replied. "Go and visit father, and I will watch the strangers."

"Where is he? Where is that wretched Greek?" Poseidon screamed. His rage shook the earth and created stormy seas.

Athena just smiled. She knew where Odysseus was. Her owl of wisdom was keeping an eye on him. After heading north, he followed the coastline. Poseidon thought he was in the Western Sea, and that's where he was looking for him. Athena knew Odysseus had just crossed over to the Eastern Sea. Poseidon wasn't looking there, and none of the Olympians were going to tell him anything different. They were tired of his bouts of anger and temper tantrums.

What she didn't understand was why he stopped on Thrinacian. They were almost home. With just a few days sailing, they would be safe. *Don't delay, Odysseus*, she thought. *Head straight home. You're almost there*.

"Where is he?" Poseidon raged again. "I'll find that wandering Greek, and then he'll suffer!"

"Wandering Greek?" A voice came from the other room. Poseidon stopped and stared. It was Phaethusa, Helios's daughter. She didn't spend much time on Mount Olympus, so she didn't know about Poseidon's vendetta against Odysseus. She was about to leave when she heard Poseidon ranting about some Greek. "We just had some Greek strangers land on Thrinacian. You don't mean them, do you?"

Poseidon became silent and rushed to the other side of Mount Olympus. "That's him!" he screamed. He was about to raise his trident and strike when he heard a voice.

"Stop, brother!" Poseidon turned around. It was Zeus. "You cannot harm anything on the island. Helios's cattle are protected."

"But Odysseus is there. You said I could have vengeance on him for his insults."

"That is true, but he is on Thrinacian. You can't harm him while he's on the island."

"But my vengeance!"

"That's your problem, brother. You cannot harm him while he's on the island!" Then Zeus turned and left.

Poseidon fumed. Zeus had tied his hands. Then he thought for a moment. *Yes*, he thought. *That will work. I'll be rid of Odysseus, and he will do the work for me.*

With that he waved his trident.

The next morning, the Greeks were preparing to leave on Thrinacian when a large storm suddenly appeared and surrounded the island. The island itself was peaceful, but the storm around it was so violent that the seas just a few yards off the beach were too rough to sail. They weren't going anywhere.

"I'm not worried, sire," Eurylochus tried to say with a smug attitude, but Odysseus detected a nervousness in his voice. "The storm will pass in a few days."

"A large storm that surrounds an island but the weather over the land remains fair?" Odysseus replied. "Does that sound like a normal storm to you, Eurylochus?"

When Eurylochus didn't reply, Odysseus simply walked away.

The Greeks had plenty of supplies when they landed, but days soon turned into weeks. After two weeks, the Greeks' supplies ran low. After three, they ran out. There was no game on the island, and the waters were too rough to fish, so the Greeks began to starve. After twenty-eight days, Odysseus's men asked him what they should do.

"I will make a plea to Zeus to lift the storm and allow us to leave," Odysseus told them. "But before I leave, everyone must again promise not to harm the cattle of Helios." Every man did, and Odysseus left and climbed a large hill. It was nightfall before he reached the top to make his plea to the King of the Olympians.

"Father," Athena said. "Look at brave, Odysseus. He and his men have been trapped on Thrinacian. They are without food and are beginning to starve. I ask you to have Poseidon lift the storm and allow them to leave."

Zeus was getting tired of his brethren's tantrums as much as the other Olympians, but he wasn't about to let Odysseus off the hook. "Daughter, Odysseus is brave and just, but there is trouble amongst his men. I cannot come to the aid of men who do not show loyalty to their leader when he gives it to them. I will test his men. I will put Odysseus into a deep sleep, and if his men can last the day without causing harm, then I will fill their ships with meat, cheese, honey, and water and allow them to return home."

After Odysseus made his plea, Zeus placed him into a deep sleep. When he didn't return in the morning, Eurylochus began to make trouble. He called the crew together to address them.

"Once again, our king has led us to disaster," he began. "We are stranded on this island facing the slow agonizing death of starvation. There is something we can do, but he is afraid to take that bold step. Look around everyone. There are cattle everywhere. Animals that can feed all of us. Animals that can nourish us. If we are bold, none of us has to starve."

"We have been warned not to harm the cattle of Helios," someone cried. "If we do, we will die."

"I have a plan that will protect us," Eurylochus replied. "We take the best cattle, slaughter them, and offer them as gifts to the other Olympians. That way they will see us as honoring them and will keep Helios from punishing us. With Helios in check, we will be able eat the smaller, weakest animals without fear of punishment."

"What if you're wrong?" another replied.

"Then we die a quick and honorable death," Eurylochus said. "It's better to have a quick death in battle than face the slow death of starvation."

The men looked at each other. They were delirious from lack of food and not thinking correctly. Before long, they all agreed with Eurylochus and began slaughtering the cattle.

The next morning, Odysseus woke from his sleep and returned to his men. He was shocked at what he saw. All along the beach were fires and what looked like beef cooking over them. "Eurylochus! What have you done?"

"The men were starving, sire. We had to do something. But not to worry, I have a plan to save us all." Then he'd told him of his plan.

Odysseus was dumbfounded. "Do you seriously believe the Olympians will be fooled by this? They will strike you down for this insult."

Then Odysseus turned to his men. "Men, you have done a foolish thing. Stop what you're doing and beg the Olympians for forgiveness and accept their punishment. It's the only way to keep them from striking you down!"

"They haven't done anything to us so far," Eurylochus replied smugly. They handed Odysseus some meat. "Here, now enjoy some meat."

Odysseus refused and walked away. He wasn't the only one who saw what happened. Lampetia also saw what the Greeks had done. She raced to Mount Olympus to tell her father.

"I demand full payment for this insult!" Helios cried. "They must pay for this with their lives!"

For once, it wasn't Poseidon screaming about how he had been wronged. Normally Helios was rather reserved, but he considered his cattle a prized possession.

He continued. "These magnificent beasts do not reproduce, so they cannot be replaced. The Greeks were warned and promised their king they wouldn't harm them. Now they have gone back on their word. They even tried to fool us by offering the best cattle as a gift to the Olympians."

All of the Olympians saw through Eurylochus's ruse. None of them accepted the gift. *Oh Odysseus*, Athena thought, *what have your men done*? She couldn't say anything or help him in any way, not for something this blatant. Trying to fool them by offering the best cattle as a gift? That was an insult to all the Olympians including her. She had to go along with what was about to happen.

Helios continued. "If I'm not paid in full, I will take the sun and shine it in the underworld!"

"You will do no such thing," Zeus told him. "You will be avenged, but I will administer the punishment."

Athena could do nothing. They had fallen into Poseidon's trap. Now they had to pay.

For days, Odysseus's men enjoyed the fresh meat without any apparent punishment. Eurylochus was certain his plan had worked. But there were other signs. Hides began to move, and the meat moaned ever so softly even when it was being cooked. Eurylochus took this as a sign the Olympians were pleased with them. Odysseus wasn't convinced and refused to eat any.

On the sixth day, the weather broke, and the skies cleared. "See, everyone!" Eurylochus declared. "My plan worked! The Olympians have shown us good favor by lifting the storm. Now we can leave and return home!"

Odysseus had the men set sail. *Go ahead, Odysseus*, Eurylochus thought. *Lead the men. They all know I saved them. In a couple of days, we will do away with you, and I will lead the men home in triumph.*

As they rowed away from the island, a large, dark storm cloud appeared on the horizon. Then it moved directly over them. It was not a typical storm. The oceans under the cloud were violent, but the waters elsewhere were calm. It was clear that the storm was targeting them. The winds were driving them west, away from home. Odysseus knew the punishment of the Olympians was at hand.

As the clouds grew darker, the seas grew more violent. Then a large, ominous figure appeared on top of the cloud. Everyone knew it was Zeus. Odysseus remained calm as panic gripped the ship. The men watched as Zeus raised his arm. He had something white and jagged in his hand. "IT`S A THUNDERBOLT!" someone yelled. Zeus let loose his thunderbolt. It struck them mid-ship destroying their vessel. Odysseus was thrown into the water. When he surfaced, there was only wreckage. Zeus was gone, but the storm was still there driving them west, away from home.

"Men!" Odysseus screamed. "Is there anyone out there?" Odysseus hoped that if he survived, then maybe others did to. "Eurylochus! Alkimos! Amphidamas! Anyone!" He thought he heard voices but couldn't tell who they were.

As the storm continued, he pulled together wreckage. Poles, planks, scrap wood, rope. Anything that would float or hold things together. After several hours, he fashioned a raft from the wreckage. Exhausted, he climbed on board and continued his search for survivors. "Men! If you can hear me, swim this way! I've built a raft! It's our best chance for survival!"

Odysseus searched for several hours as the winds blew him west. He thought he heard voices, but the storm created waves and a heavy spray that obscured his vision. He could not see anyone. Then he spied a distant shore off to the west. As it drew closer, there appeared to be a passage between two bodies of land. Odysseus thought their ordeal may be over until he saw a large cliff. On top of the cliff was a large fig tree in full bloom.

Charybdis! The storm had blown directly over Charybdis. When the waters began to swirl, Odysseus realized she was beginning to drink. He knew the whirlpool would form and suck everything down. He thought his life was over when he saw something on the side of the cliff. Through the mist, he could see that a large root from the fig tree had grown through the cliff and was out above the water. As the water began to swirl, it pulled his raft toward the root. Odysseus knew he had only one chance for survival. When his raft was below the root, he leapt with the last of his strength. He grabbed hold of the root and pulled himself out of the water just as the whirlpool formed. He was safe.

Odysseus turned and looked at the whirlpool. It drew in everything: wreckage, his raft, fish, and any survivors. He winced with pain. He knew from Circe that Charybdis would drink for hours, and he wasn't sure how long he could hold on. He tried to look at the root, but it was covered in a thick mist. A strange pain developed in his hands as he hung there.

As dawn broke, the storm ended, and the whirlpool began to subside. When it stopped, a huge spout of water appeared. Charybdis was spitting out what she couldn't digest. Odysseus looked and saw that Charybdis had spit out his raft. He let go of the root, swam to the raft, and began paddling east. When the whirlpool formed again, he was too far away to be drawn in. He paddled a few more hours before passing out from exhaustion.

Of six hundred men and twelve ships that left Troy with Odysseus, all that was left was one man on a raft made of wreckage.

CHAPTER 12

CALYPSO

The young woman was walking the beach of her island. She was all alone, singing a simple song. She was the immortal daughter of the Titian Atlas who was banished here by Zeus because she sided with her father during the Olympian's war with the Titians. Hera took pity on her and occasionally sent her servants to make her life comfortable, but they didn't stay long and never talked to her. For thousands of years, she endured the loneliness imposed on her. Her name was Calypso.

It was with great surprise that Calypso found a man washed up on the beach. He was in rags, and next to him appeared to be a raft of some kind. She ran to him. Yes, he was still alive. She looked around and did not see anyone else. *He must be the only survivor of a shipwreck*, she thought. Calypso walked over to the raft and pushed it back out to sea. Then she dragged the stranger back to her home where she began to nurse him back to health.

After two days, the stranger regained consciousness. He looked around and saw he was in an ornate, well-kept cave. An equally beautiful woman was hovering over him. "Where am I?" he asked.

"You are in my home, a cave on the island of Ogygian in the Eastern Sea," she replied.

"How did I get here?"

"I found you washed up on my beach. You were unconscious, so I brought you here and nursed you back to health. That was two days ago."

"Who are you?"

"I am Calypso, daughter of the Titian Atlas."

"How did you get here?"

"I was banished here by Zeus because I supported my father during their war." Then she asked the stranger a question. "Who are you, and how did you come upon my island?"

The stranger thought for a moment. After everything he'd been through, he thought this could be a trap. But the girl had answered his questions directly and honestly. Besides, if she wanted to do him harm, she would have done it while he was unconscious. "I am Odysseus." Then he told her his tale.

After his encounter with Charybdis, he spent nine days on his makeshift raft before he came across this island where he crawled up on the beach and collapsed. "What happened to the raft?" Odysseus asked.

Calypso shrugged. "I don't know. I didn't see a raft on the beach. It must have washed out to sea."

"I want to look for it." Odysseus demanded.

Calypso leaned back and gestured to the front of the cave. As Odysseus tried to sit up, he became weak and fell back on the bed. Then she said sarcastically, "Let me know when you want to try that again. Not much on this island makes me laugh but that surely did."

Odysseus shot her an angry glance. Then she stood. "Eat and rest a few days. After you recover your strength, you can explore the island." Then she stood up and went over to her loom that had a beautiful half-finished tapestry in it. Calypso picked up her golden shuttle and sang a song as she moved to and fro weaving on her loom with a golden shuttle.

When he awoke on the morning of the second day, Odysseus was feeling stronger, but his head was dizzy. *Must be from the ordeal on the raft*, he thought. As he looked over, he saw Calypso weaving on her loom with a golden shuttle, singing as she swayed to and fro. He was about to say something when she stopped, pointed, and said, "The exit's that way."

Odysseus went outside. The island was green and relatively flat but devoid of any trees or shrubs. He walked along the beach—nothing. No wreckage, seaweed, or anything else from the sea. *Poseidon's revenge*, he thought. There was nothing on the island that he could use to make a raft let alone a boat. When he climbed a small hill on the south side of the island, he looked down and saw a strange, dark fog covering the extreme southern portion of the island. He watched it for several hours. It didn't dissipate like most fogs did when the sun rose. In fact, it never changed. He walked up to it and placed his hand in it. It was so thick that he couldn't see his hand once it entered the fog. He withdrew his hand, and it was fine.

When he returned to the cave that evening, he spoke to Calypso. "What can you tell me about this island?"

"It's a relatively flat island with some small hills," she said "It has no trees or shrubs. The weather is fair year-round." She stopped working at her loom and continued. "There is a strange fog on the south side of the island. The fog never changes, never grows larger or smaller. It's so thick that you cannot see through it. One day, I decided to see if I could pass through it. I planned on walking one hundred paces into it, and if I didn't reach the other side, I would walk backwards the same one hundred paces to exit it." A shiver came over her body as she looked at Odysseus. "I only went ten paces then stopped. I was confused because I could not see anything. I was scared, so I walked ten paces backwards to exit. I've never tried to enter the fog again."

"Do you have any tools on this island?"

"Only knives and other basic utensils."

"How do you manage?"

"Hera took pity on me. She sends servants every so often to make my life comfortable, but they don't talk to me or stay long."

Odysseus was about to ask more questions when he suddenly felt faint and started to sway. Calypso rushed to him. "OK, enough for now. Rest and eat. Then continue tomorrow."

The next day, Odysseus awoke, and again Calypso was weaving on her loom with a golden shuttle, singing as she swayed to and fro. He walked outside and continued to search for anything that could help him return to his wife and son.

His thoughts turned to them—oh how he longed to be with them. His beautiful loving wife Penelope. To touch and caress her soft hair. And his son Telemachus. He was becoming a man, and he wasn't there to guide him. The pain of not seeing them tore at his soul. It was an agony no man should bear. He had to leave this island, but he couldn't find a way. He was confused and disorientated, and it was becoming harder for him to concentrate. He ached for them, the torment increasing with every passing minute.

"Why is this happening to me?" he yelled as the pain overtook him. "I miss my wife and son. I miss Penelope's sweet caress and lovely face. I wish to see my son. This longing is unbearable!" He searched the island over and over again and still found nothing. The more he searched, the more he longed for his family and the greater the pain became. Finally, he collapsed on the hill overlooking the beach where Calypso found him and wept.

Days turned into weeks and always the same. A confused and disorientated Odysseus would leave the cave, sit on the hill overlooking the beach, and weep as he longed to be with his wife and son. His head was too dizzy to concentrate on a plan to leave this island. All he could do was weep. Then, at the end of the day, he would return to Calypso's cave where she was weaving on her loom with a golden shuttle, singing as she swayed to and fro.

One day while he was weeping, Calypso came up to him and asked, "Why are you weeping Odysseus?"

"My heart is aching, and my soul is tormented because I cannot be with my wife and son."

She put her arm around him and gave him a hug. "It will be all right, Odysseus." Then she returned to the cave.

Odysseus's torment only increased as the weeks wore on. Then one day, Calypso came to him. She put her arms around him and gently caressed him as she spoke. "Odysseus, I know you are tormented, but this can all end. I am an immortal. If you become my husband, your longing and pain will end. I will make you immortal as well, never having to face Hades and the underworld. You'll be able to forget your wife and son. Your life will be carefree and comfortable. We can start another family. All you have to do is become my husband."

"No," Odysseus said through his tears. "I must remain true to them. I must find a way to return."

Calypso said nothing more but held him for the rest of the day.

As the weeks turned into months, this became Odysseus's life on Ogygian. Every day, he would wake up, and his head would be dizzy and confused while Calypso weaved on her loom with a golden shuttle, singing as she swayed to and fro. He would eat then go to the hill overlooking the beach and weep as his heart and soul were tormented by the longing he felt for his wife and son. Every day, his longing for them would increase causing his pain to increase. Every few days, Calypso would join him and present her offer to him, and he would refuse. Then he would return to the cave for his evening meal. And there would be Calypso, weaving on her loom with a golden shuttle, singing as she swayed to and fro.

Poseidon was actually laughing. "This is perfect! Why didn't I think of this before?"

Because something like this is too subtle for a brute like you, Athena thought. In fact, he didn't even think of it at all. Poseidon lost track of Odysseus during the storm. At one point, he was happy because he thought Charybdis had devoured him. The only reason he knew Odysseus was on Ogygian was because one of the servants Hera sent to Calypso reported he was there. Athena knew he was there all the time because her owl of wisdom kept her informed.

"Calypso has cast her spell on him," Poseidon continued. "His heart aches for his wife, and the longing to be with his son is tearing his soul apart. The longer he's there, the more painful it is. A torn heart and tormented soul are a punishment worse than everything he's been through." Then he laughed again.

Athena was not amused. Zeus spared Odysseus because he didn't harm Helios's cattle, but he wasn't going to help him either. He was their leader. He lost control of his men, and they ate the cattle of Helios. That was why he was suffering on Ogygian, not because of Poseidon's plan.

Hang on Odysseus, she thought. *The day will come when I will be able to help you. But for now, you must hang on.*

CHAPTER 13

THE RETURN

"Father, may I speak with you?"

The king had many problems to deal with. Sometimes it took all his patience not to lose his temper, but he always loved talking with his first born. She wasn't petty like the rest. She could lose her temper—that was a fact—but only for a valid reason. She was his favorite, and it was always a joy to speak with her. Zeus turned, looked at his daughter, and smiled. "Yes, Athena, I always have time for you."

"For seven years, Odysseus has been held prisoner on Ogygian by the seductress Calypso," Athena said. "She has fallen in love with him, but he has not returned her love. She has cast her spell on him so that he is confused and can't think clearly. She has forced him to become her lover. All Odysseus wishes to do is return to his wife and son. This longing is tearing apart his heart and tormenting his spirit. She tempts him with immortality if he becomes her husband, but he refuses. Yes, Odysseus has done wrong. He blinded Polyphemus, insulted Poseidon, and allowed his men to eat the cattle of Helios. But seven years of torment at the hands of Calypso is enough punishment for one man to bear. Odysseus should be allowed to leave Ogygian and continue his journey home."

Zeus was the wisest of the Olympians. He alone knew what Athena did to Lamos before Odysseus arrived and how she had her brother Hermes help him with Circe. Zeus smiled to himself at the one, a trickster outsmarting another trickster. She had been helping Odysseus during his journey—with Aeolus, Scylla, and Charybdis. He knew his daughter was championing Odysseus's cause, and she was presenting her case now was because Poseidon was away at a festival in Ethiopia.

Zeus said nothing, of course, because he admired her cleverness and deception. His daughter had done these things under the very nose of Poseidon, a remarkable feat to be sure. She was a crafty and clever one indeed. Still, her arguments were just and correct. Odysseus had made mistakes and needed to be punished, but seven years of heartache was more than enough punishment for any mortal. He smiled, "I will call an assembly of the Olympians this afternoon, and you can present your case to them."

Athena presented her case at the assembly. While before them all, Athena looked at her brother Hermes. He was smiling because he figured out her plan as well. The other Olympians also agreed—seven years of torment was enough punishment for any mortal. It also helped that they were tired of Poseidon's outbursts and gloating over Odysseus's plight. The decision was made. It was time for Calypso to allow Odysseus to leave Ogygian. When they all agreed, Zeus called on Hermes to deliver the message to Calypso.

It was the afternoon when Hermes arrived at Calypso's cave. Odysseus was on the hill at the beach weeping while Calypso was weaving on her loom with a golden shuttle, singing as she swayed to and fro. "You can stop your enchantress song, Calypso," he said. "I have a message from Zeus."

Calypso did not care for Zeus or any other Olympian for that matter. He was the one who banished her here. She turned. "What does the almighty Zeus, King of the Olympians, want with the lowly daughter of a Titian?" she said in a mocking voice. "I thought he would have more important things to worry about in that lofty palace of his."

"I would hold my tongue if I were you, Calypso," he warned. "There are far worse punishments Zeus can give you." Then he continued. "Zeus has commanded that you release Odysseus from your spell and allow him to leave this island."

Calypso was furious. "Why should I? You Olympian men take female mortals as your lovers all the time. None of you have ever had to release them. You yourself are Odysseus's great grandfather. The hypocrisy of you Olympians knows no bounds. You take what you want and then deny the same for the rest of us. Why should I release him? Because I'm a woman? Why can't I have the same pleasures as you and the others?"

"Odysseus longs to return to his wife and son," Hermes replied. "For seven years he has refused your offer of immortality if he becomes your husband even though you have forced him to be your lover with your enchanting songs. He has not returned your love, and he is not yours to take. Now release him as Zeus commands."

Then Hermes left. Tears formed in Calypso's eyes. She remembered what Zeus did to the other Titians after the war. If she disobeyed him, she could find herself in Tartarus facing the same torments as them. She could even face a punishment worse than her fathers. She was in love with Odysseus, but now she had to let him go. Calypso fell on her knees and wept.

On the hill overlooking the beach, Odysseus was also weeping. He longed for his wife and son, but he couldn't concentrate. His head was dizzy and confused. Suddenly, his head began to clear. He knew what he had to do. He had to leave. He had to return to them. He was energized at that thought. Somehow, he was going to get off this island even if he had to swim to Ithica.

He stood and turned to see Calypso next to him. "This way," she said as she motioned to the south. He followed her to the hill overlooking the south side of the island. When she reached the top, she gestured to the other side. As Odysseus reached the top, he looked down. The strange dark fog that covered the south part of the island was gone. Before him stood trees, thousands of them. More than enough to make a boat. He also saw a large stone building.

Next to him, Odysscus heard Calypso speak. "Inside the building, you will find everything you need to build a raft or boat. Tools, planks, fasteners, rope, sail, everything. The trees are fine, stout trees, excellent building material for ships."

Odysseus took a few steps forward. He was dumbfounded. Here was everything he needed to return home. It had been covered by the fog while something made his head dizzy and confused. He suspected sorcery, but when he turned to confront Calypso, she was gone.

He didn't have time to look for her. Odysseus entered the stone building. Just as Calypso said, everything he needed to build a boat was here. He got to work. For five days, Odysseus worked without sleep—cutting, carving, fastening, making a sail, hauling, whatever was needed. He built his boat on the beach below the hill where he wept for so many years. When he was finished, he had a one-man sailboat that could handle the high seas. He filled his boat with supplies and was ready to leave.

Before Odysseus left, he took one last look at the hill where he spent so many years weeping as he longed for his family. At the top of the hill was Calypso standing there with sadness and grief on her face. Most men would be angry with her; they would even try to kill her. Odysseus didn't. He felt sadness for her. As someone who understood the pain of loneliness, he understood what she was feeling. Through all his trials he faced on his journey, the trials of loneliness were the most tragic. He had suffered that pain for seven years while she had been suffering it for thousands of years. Now after a brief respite, she was going to feel that pain again. He knew she loved him, but he could never return her love. Without saying a word, he entered his boat and sailed away.

As Odysseus left, Calypso raised her hand. A fair breeze filled his sail taking him home to Ithaca. It was the last thing she could do for lost love.

Odysseus wasn't the only one on his way home. Poseidon was riding the seas in his magnificent chariot pulled by a pair of Hippocamps. He was returning to Mount Olympus from his trip to Ethiopia. His spirits were high when he noticed a small one-man sailboat off in the distance. *That's odd*, he thought. *Who is this daring sailor who is brave enough to travel the high seas by himself?* As he drew closer, he was shocked to see who it was. "Odysseus!" he screamed. *How did he escape Calypso's island?* Now he was only a day sailing from Ithaca. Poseidon raised his trident. He didn't care about the Fates as he raised a storm to destroy him once and for all. The storm threw Odysseus into the sea and sank his boat. Poseidon moved in for the kill but could not find him. Where was Odysseus? Where was he?

"Odysseus where are you?" he cried.

CHAPTER 14

THE PHAEACIANS

T he princess and her servants were playing ball on the beach while their clothes dried. Her name was Nausicaä, the daughter of Alcinous and Aretthe, King and Queen of the Phaeacians. She was a young girl but wise beyond her years. Last night, she had a strange dream calling for her and her servants to wash their clothes in the river by the beach this morning. A strange dream to be sure, but she thought it might help her find a suitor. If her parents knew what she was doing, they might not agree. As they came to a clump of trees, they heard a voice. "Please don't come any closer."

Nausicaä was surprised. This beach was supposed to be empty. "Hello stranger, who are you?" she said as they retrieved their clothes.

The stranger spoke from the trees. He was careful to hide his true identity. "A shipwreck survivor who is on his way home," he said. "Unfortunately, I lost my clothes in the storm."

Nausicaä signaled for her servants to bring the stranger some clothes. "You better stop speaking in riddles stranger, or I'll call my guards and they'll run you through."

After dressing, the stranger stepped out of the trees. "I'm a nobleman on my way home and in need of help. If you are of royalty, I humbly request your hospitality to help me on my journey."

Nausicaä thought for a moment before speaking. "Very well, nobleman returning home, if that's who you are. I will take you before my parents, and you can plead your case. I warn you, though, that they do not suffer fools. If you're not who you say you are, it will be a swift trip to the underworld for you."

That afternoon, the well-dressed stranger stood before the King and Queen. "So stranger, you claim to be a nobleman returning from Troy," King Alcinous said.

"Yes, your Grace," the stranger replied.

"Where are you traveling to and from?"

"I am traveling to Greece from Troy, your Grace."

"Did you serve in the Trojan War?"

"Yes, your Grace."

"Then you should know things about the other nobleman who served there as well. When was the last time Odysseus saw his wife Clytemnestra, son Orestes and daughter Electra?"

"Those people are not from Odysseus's family, your Grace."

"Yes, that's right. They were the family of Achilles, a good friend of your general Hector."

"Hector was a Trojan prince killed by Achilles, your Grace. Clytemnestra, Orestes, and Electra were the family of Agamemnon." Then, before King Alcinous could say another word, the stranger continued. "And before you ask, your Grace, Agamemnon and Achilles did not like each other."

The stranger continued. "Odysseus's wife is Penelope. His son is Telemachus, and he has no daughter." Suddenly the stranger knelt and began to weep.

"What is the matter, stranger?" King Alcinous asked.

Through the tears in his eyes, the stranger found the courage to speak. "I am Odysseus, King of Ithaca, your Grace. It has been twenty years since I've seen my family, and my heart longs for them. It's all I can do to bear the pain of missing them."

King Alcinous nodded. "How did you come to our land?"

"It's a long story, your Grace," Odysseus replied. A long story indeed. He had been at sea eighteen days after leaving Ogygian when a storm suddenly appeared. Odysseus suspected Poseidon was behind it. The storm sank his ship and would have drowned him if the sea immortal Ino hadn't loaned him a veil to keep him afloat and hide him from Poseidon. Somehow, he avoided the rocks and washed ashore on this beach. He returned the veil to the sea, but the storm also cost him everything, including his clothes.

After Odysseus finished, King Alcinous smiled. "I suspected as much, Odysseus. But there is one way for sure to make sure you are who you say you are." He motioned to an attendant. An old man walked into the room.

"This is a bard who use to be in the service of Menelaus, King of Sparta. The tale of the Trojan horse was told to him by Menelaus, and he has told it to me. He will begin the tale, nobleman, and if you are Odysseus, you will be able to end it."

The bard had barely begun the story when Odysseus finished it. He told King Alcinous how Agamemnon approached him because they could not take Troy by force. How forty of them, including Menelaus, hid in the wooden horse without armor, their swords and shield wrapped in hides. Anyone who uttered a sound would have their throats slit. That night when they exited the horse, they found themselves just inside the main gate. He told how he signaled Menelaus to have his men dispatch the four guards standing watch then had his Spartans form a line in case they were discovered. And finally, how they opened the gates and were ready to disable the gears if they were discovered so even if they were killed, the gates couldn't be closed. That night when the Greek army returned, they rushed in and slaughtered the Trojans as they celebrated their supposed victory.

After he finished his story of the Trojan horse, he continued on with the journey of his return—the Cicones, Lotus Eaters, the cyclops, Areolas, the Laestergoins, Circe, the land of the dead, Poseidon, the Sirens, Scylla and Charybdis, Helios's cattle, Calypso, and finally ending with his shipwreck here.

After Odysseus finished his story, King Alcinous rose. "Thank you, King Odysseus of Ithaca. Please accept our hospitality. We will provide you with food, drink, passage to Ithaca, and more treasure that you would have collected from Troy. We are a prosperous country, and this is the least we can do for someone who has been through so much and suffered so terribly."

"Your Grace, I must warn you," Odysseus said, "if you help me, you may incur the wrath of Poseidon."

"Yes, that is true," King Alcinous said. "Poseidon is a difficult Olympian to be sure, but we have dealt with his anger before. The tradition of hospitality compels us to help you, so we will help you now then appease Poseidon should he bring disaster to our land."

Over the next several days, there was a great celebration honoring Odysseus. When it was over, a ship sailed taking him to Ithaca. He was dropped off at night to make sure Poseidon did not find him before he returned. They dressed him as a common laborer to hide his identity. Then the ship sailed away.

Finally, after twenty years, Odysseus had returned to Ithaca.

CHAPTER 15

The Reunion

A s morning came, Odysseus found himself in a thick mist with his treasure beside him. He disguised it as best he could and then started up a path. Along the way, he met a young shepherd girl.

"Hello, stranger," the shepherd girl said. "You're new around here. Are you looking for work?"

"Yes, I am. I was hoping to find work in the house of Odysseus. I have strong hands and am able to do most anything."

"There is great turmoil there, stranger," the girl replied. "Many suitors are trying to force the Queen to marry one of them. They claim her husband is dead, and they are trying to steal his throne, but she has been loyal to him the entire time he has been away. Maybe you should try elsewhere. There are many estates around here where you can find employment."

"No, I must find work in the Manor House."

"Where are you from?"

"I just arrived from the Phaeacians."

The girl nodded. "Yes, I here there is great turmoil there as well. They say Alcinous helped Odysseus and has earned Poseidon's wrath."

Odysseus sensed something. How did this shepherd girl know so much? How did she know about the suitors? He just landed here, so how could she know about King Alcinous helping him? How could she know Poseidon was angry with the Phaeacians for helping him? Why didn't she use the term King when speaking about him or King Alcinous? He decided to take a chance. He threw away his laborers disguise. "I can assure you I must go to the Manor House because I am Odysseus, King of Ithaca."

The shepherd girl smiled. "I know who you are, Odysseus." Then a glow appeared around the girl as she revealed herself, a young woman dressed in full armor and carrying weapons.

Odysseus took a knee when he saw her. "Olympian Athena," was all he could say.

"Rise," Athena said with a smile. "It is good to see you after your long and difficult journey." Then she looked at him. "Rest assured, Odysseus, I have never left your side and have done everything I could to help you."

She began by describing how Poseidon was angry with him for blinding his son Polyphemus and mocking him. After Poseidon's storms forced them into the Western Sea, she gently moved Aeolus's floating island into his path. When he was sailing towards Lamos, the island of the Laestergoins, she shrank the lagoon so it would be too small to hold all of the ships, and one ship—his ship—would have to remain outside. How she convinced Hermes to help him with Circe. When it was time to face Scylla, she made sure Crataeis would hear his plea and prevent her daughter from string a second time. How her owl of wisdom kept an eye on him as he traveled along the northern route. When he was hanging onto the root over Charybdis, she gave her owl of wisdom great strength, hid him in the mist, and had him hold Odysseus's hands together so that he couldn't let go. She went to Zeus while Poseidon was away and convinced him to allow Odysseus to leave Calypso's island. When Poseidon sank his ship, she helped him avoid the rocks and make it to shore. Finally, she was the one who gave Princess Nausicaä the dream to do her laundry in the river by the beach."

"I never thought you had abandoned me, Olympian Athena," Odysseus said.

"I have also helped your family as well, Odysseus," Athena said.

During his absence, Athena visited his son Telemachus in many forms: as an instructor, a mentor, and a friend. She made sure that he grew up into an honorable and just young man. She also protected him from the attempts by the suitors to kill him. The last thing Athena did was send him on a journey of discovery to find out the fate of his father. First to Nestor, king of Pylos, who fought with Odysseus during the Trojan war. Next to Sparta to visit King Menelaus who was with Odysseus in the Trojan Horse. From these men he learned that his father was alive.

In addition, Athena gave his wife Penelope visions that her husband was alive and that she should wait for him. Penelope never wavered and was always faithful to him. For years, she kept the suitors at bay waiting for him to return.

After they talked, Athena helped Odysseus hide his treasure in a cave that only he could find. Then she turned to him. "Odysseus, time is short. The Fates declared that you would return, and now that you have, there is nothing to stop Poseidon from killing you. Right now, he is more interested in punishing the Phaeacians for helping you, so you must act quickly."

"Go to the farmhouse of Eumaeus, your swine header. He has been loyal to you and will help you regain your house from the suitors." Then she smiled. "You will also meet your son there as well." Then she disappeared.

Odysseus rushed to Eumaeus's farmhouse. When he arrived, his old servant couldn't believe what he saw. "Sire!" he exclaimed. "Is it really you or have I descended into madness!"

"It is I," Odysseus replied. "After twenty years, I have returned." As they embraced, they heard a knock at the door. When Eumaeus opened the door, Odysseus saw a young man in his early twenties, healthy and vibrant, standing in the entrance way.

A lump formed in his throat. This moment made the twenty years of war, pain, sorrow, and torment bearable. His family was the reason he endured such hardship, was willing to face any challenge, and was what gave him the strength to return home. Seeing his son now was like looking into a mirror except for the few soft features of his mother. He was someone Odysseus hadn't seen since he was an infant. Odysseus slowly walked over to the youth.

"Son," was all Odysseus managed to say. "Is that you my dear Telemachus?"

Telemachus looked at the stranger. He had received a vision to come here tonight. "Have we met, kind sir?"

Athena did an excellent job raising the boy, Odysseus thought. *He is courteous but not afraid.* "Not for twenty years. I am your father Odysseus."

Telemachus did not believe him until Athena showed Odysseus in his full glory. "Father!" he exclaimed. The two embraced and cried. After the joyous reunion, Eumaeus suggested they enlist the aid of Philoetius, Odysseus's loyal cow header. Together the four of them came up with a plan for Odysseus to defeat the invaders trying to seal his wife and his throne.

CHAPTER 16

THE SUITORS

T he beggar approached the Manor House. Beggars had always been given hospitality at this house, and Odysseus was counting on that to gain entrance. With Athena's help, he disguised himself well. Athena shriveled his skin and aged his looks while Eumaeus and Philoetius gave him filthy rags so that none would recognize him.

But there was one he could not fool. As he approached the front of the house, Odysseus spied his faithful dog, Argo. He had remained there since Odysseus left, and when he saw his master return, he sat up and gave him a warm greeting, grateful to see him again. Then he passed away. *Rest easy, old friend*, Odysseus thought. *You shall know peace after waiting so many years for my return.*

As Odysseus approached his house, he remembered what Telemachus, Eumaeus, and

Philoetius told him. Several years after receiving the news of their victory over Troy, Odysseus had not returned home. Without any word from him, the people began to believe he was dead. It wasn't long before men began to approach his wife demanding her hand in marriage. As time went on, more and more approached until one hundred and eight of them began to call his house home. They called themselves suitors, but, in reality, they were swine—dishonorable men violating the tradition of hospitality, spending his fortune, disrespecting Penelope, destroying his home, and acting as if his absence was a cause for celebration. Soon, many of his servants were joining them. Eumaeus and Philoetius tried to force them to leave, but there were just too many of them. To keep peace amongst themselves, the suitors agreed to keep all their weapons in a corner of the banquet hall. That way no single suitor could plot treachery and kill the others while they were in a drunken state.

Penelope held the suitors at bay for several years. First, she said she could never marry until her son grew facial hair. Afterwards, she claimed she could not marry anyone until she finished weaving a burial shroud for her husband's elderly father, Laertes. Every morning, she would weave the shroud, and every night she would undo everything she did in the morning.

This worked for several years until their maid Melantho, who was a lover of one of the suitors, revealed the deception. Now Penelope was forced to choose someone to be her husband to prevent open warfare from breaking out across the land.

Odysseus approached the door and knocked. When a servant opened it, Odysseus began to speak. "Kind servant, I am but a humble beggar asking for the generous hospitality from the house of Odysseus—a night's stay, a good meal, and a bed for the night,and then allow me to continue on my way."

"Our King has not yet returned, but our Queen still holds to his tradition," the servant said. They motioned for Odysseus to enter and led him to the banquet hall. The situation was far worse that Telemachus described.

The banquet hall was filthy. It had not been cleaned in years. Dirt and filth were everywhere. Dirt, food, and spilled drinks were all over the floors and tables. The suitors were lounging around everywhere in a drunken state. Twelve of his servants were with them, celebrating, as if there wasn't a care in the world. "Hey look," one of them yelled. "We have another dreg looking for a free handout. Let's see if he moves faster than the last one." The man threw a stool at Odysseus. After ten years of dodging Trojan spears, he easily avoided the stool.

Laughter came from the other suitors. "Looks like you need more practice, Antinous!" someone yelled. "Mind you own business, Eurymachus!" Antinous yelled back. Odysseus remembered what his son told him about these two. Antinous was the most arrogant of the suitors. Eurymachus was a manipulative, deceitful suitor who seemed to be their leader.

Eurymachus walked up to him. "Well, grease ball," he sneered, "in order to eat here, you have to earn your keep. Irus!" Another large bulky beggar approached. "Only one of you can be here, so whoever can best the other can stay." Without another word, he backed away.

Irus approached Odysseus. "Leave now before I break your neck!" Odysseus stood his ground. Then Irus lunged at him, but Odysseus dodged his attack. It wasn't much of a fight. Before long, Odysseus had broken Irus's jaw and thrown him out of the house.

"Congratulations, stranger!" one of the suitors said as he put his arm around Odysseus. "Come—eat, drink, and be merry! Today we celebrate your victory!"

This must be Amphinomus, Odysseus thought. The only suitor who had any kind of sense and courtesy. *I'll give him a chance*. "Good sir, you are kind and generous," Odysseus said. "I beg you to honor the good name of our king and leave this wretched bunch and return to your honorable family."

Amphinomus looked at him and laughed. "I think not," he said as he walked away and rejoined the festivities.

Next Eurymachus approached Odysseus and began to insult him. Little did he realize that trading insults with someone as quick witted as Odysseus was a losing proposition. It wasn't long before he became frustrated at being outsmarted by the master trickster. "You scum!" he yelled. "I'll teach you who is the better man!" Then Eurymachus threw a stool at him. Odysseus dodged this stool as well, but it hit a servant causing a brawl to breakout amongst the suitors.

"Enough!" came a cry from the entrance. It was Telemachus. He waded into the brawl, pulling the men apart. "Is this how you plan on winning the hand of my mother? How do you plan on ruling this land? You're not fit to rule yourselves, let alone Ithaca!" Slowly but surely, he regained control and restored order.

"Enough of this nonsense!" came a voice from the grand entrance.

Odysseus turned around and saw the most beautiful thing he had ever seen. More beautiful than Aphroditie and more graceful than Hera. The sight took his breath away. He couldn't speak. His heart raced and pulse quickened. It was all he could do to restrain himself, to keep from running to her and embracing her. The pain he endured over the decades was washed away when she appeared. It felt like he had never left Ithica. After twenty years, she still carried herself with beauty, grace, and dignity. She was and always would be the one true love of his life, his wife Penelope.

"Penelope, you must choose," Eurymachus said. "If you don't, there will be chaos."

Penelope slowly entered the room. "In honor of the Olympian Apollo, there will be an archery contest." A murmur came from the suitors. "But this will only happen if all of you promise upon the Olympians to let anyone present attempt the challenge without interference, threats, or harm. If just one of you refuses, there will be no contest."

After some discussion, all of the suitors agreed. "Very well," she said. "The contest will begin tomorrow morning." Then she motioned for one of her attendants to bring the beggar to her. The last thing Odysseus heard before leaving the banquet hall were the suitors bragging how they were going to win Penelope's hand.

When Odysseus first entered the Manor House, he talked to the servants about the Trojan War and told them about their king's exploits hoping it would lead to a meeting with his wife.

The attendants lead Odysseus to a room with his beloved wife. He refused to look directly at her because he feared he would weep at the sight of her beauty. "I understand you knew my husband," she asked.

"Yes, My Lady."

"Many claim that he is dead," she said. "I do not. I believe he will return and save our kingdom." Then she looked at him. "What can you tell me of his return?"

Odysseus remembered what Agamemnon's spirt told him. He told her of his adventures but did not burden her with the heartache. "Fear not, My Lady," he said. "Your husband will return to you and your son."

"I truly hope so," she said. "It has been hard on our family and our land. He is the only one who can restore order to our household. My heart aches for his return." Then she signaled to an older woman. "This is Eurycleia, my husband's old nursemaid. She will bath you and provide you with a warm bed."

Odysseus bowed. "I need no bed, My Lady. The floor will do nicely." With that Penelope left.

Eurycleia took Odysseus to another room. As she drew him a bath, she noticed a scar on his thigh. She knew this scar. It was from a boar wound he received when he was young. "My king!" she exclaimed.

"Yes, Eurycleia," he said. "It is I, Odysseus, and I have returned."

"My king, what can I do to serve you?"

"You can keep this secret. Tomorrow we will regain our kingdom, but only if we surprise these swine. The odds will be long, but it's our only chance. Do not tell my wife. We can't risk her giving away our secret by accident. I will need your help for what is about to happen tomorrow." Then he told her what was required. Eurycleia nodded, and then she left.

That night was a long night for Odysseus and his wife. Penelope feared she may have to choose a new husband tomorrow before her husband returned. Odysseus feared his plan may not work, and if it didn't, all would be lost.

No matter the outcome, both knew the issue with the suitors would be settled tomorrow morning.

CHAPTER 17

THE FINAL BATTLE

When morning came, all the suitors gathered in the banquet hall. With them were the twelve disloyal servants. At the front were twelve axe heads lined up in a row next to a quiver of arrows. Odysseus, still disguised as a beggar, was there along with Telemachus, Eumaeus, and Philoetius. The suitors were drinking and becoming impatient waiting for Penelope to arrive. *Good*, Odysseus thought. *The more they drink, the better for us.*

They did not have to wait long. Penelope entered wearing an elegant dress. Her attendants and Eurycleia were with her. One of her attendants was carrying a large bow. Then she began to speak. "The contest is simple. Whoever can string my husband's bow and shoot an arrow through the twelve axe heads will win my hand in marriage."

"I will go first," Telemachus said. He reached for the bow and tried four times, nearly succeeding on his fourth attempt.

Odysseus understood his son's plan. If he could win the contest, he could claim victory and prevent his mother from marrying one of these rogues. He was proud of his son for his bravery, but he knew the suitors would simply kill him the next day and then force Penelope to marry one of them anyway. He walked up to his son, put his hand on his shoulder, and said, "You are a brave one, Young Prince, but you must let things play out as they must."

With that, Telemachus returned the bow and stepped back. The suitors took this as a sign that the beggar supported their claim to the throne. Seeing how close he came to stringing the bow emboldened them. "Yes, young imp," one of them yelled, "stand back and let a real man win the contest."

The first to try was Eurymachus. He snatched the bow and tried to string it but failed. The next to try was Antinous followed by Amphinomus. For several hours the suitors tried and failed to string the bow. Many of them tried multiple times, but no matter how many attempts they made, none of them could string his bow.

"This is outrageous!" Eurymachus yelled as he threw the bow across the room. "This is just another one of your tricks, Penelope! Just like you shroud. You must choose one of us now or suffer the consequences!" A great murmur arose for the suitors.

"I'd like to try," came a voice from the back. The room became silent as the suitors turned around and realized it had come from the beggar. "I'd like to try and string the bow, My Lady."

The suitors were shocked. If the beggar strung the bow, he would humiliate them all, and then no one would accept their claim to the throne. Eurymachus approached him. "Do not test our patience or good will, scum bag. You are nothing and have no right to take part in this contest."

"Remember your promise," Penelope reminded them. "All of you promised upon the Olympians to let anyone who is present attempt the challenge without interference, threats, or harm. If you go back on your promise, the Olympians will render you senseless."

The suitors knew she was right. If any of them violated their Olympian promise, they would be punished. They all stepped back to give the beggar a chance.

Odysseus walked over and picked up the bow. Then he slowly carried it to the front of the room. All of the suitors scowled at him, but none of them said a word or interfered. Then he looked around acting as if he were confused. Telemachus,

Eumaeus, and Philoetius were all in position. They slowly nodded, signaling that they were ready.

Suddenly, like a flash of Zeus's thunderbolts, Odysseus strung the bow on the first attempt, grabbed one of the arrows from the quiver, and easily sent it through all twelve axe heads. Then he turned to the suitors and threw off his beggar's disguise while Athena restored him to his full glory. "IT'S ODYSSEUS!" Eurymachus yelled.

Odysseus looked at Eurycleia and yelled, "Get my Queen to safety!"

Penelope's attendants were in shock, but Eurycleia was ready. "Yes, sire!" she yelled as she pushed Penelope out the banquet hall door and sealed it behind her.

The suitors raced for their weapons but found they weren't there. As part of their plan, Telemachus had removed them during the night. As they tried to make sense of what was happening, they saw Telemachus, Eumaeus, and Philoetius retrieve the weapons and shields they hid in the banquet room the night before. The suitors raced toward the exits but found they were blocked by Eumaeus and Philoetius. They looked back at Odysseus who had retrieved the quiver and was readying another arrow. It was a trap, and there was nothing they could do.

Antinous was the first to die, shot through the heart by Odysseus. Agelaus soon followed.

Amphimedon was killed by Telemachus as they tried to rush the lad. Those who tried to escape through the exits were cut down by Eumaeus and Philoetius. As the battle raged, Odysseus came across Eurymachus, the leader of the group.

"No, sire, please!" Eurymachus pleaded with him. "It was Antinous! He's the one who brought us here! He was the one who lied and told everyone you were dead! He's the one who said someone should take over your throne! He's the one ..."

"Enough of you lies, swine!" Odysseus growled as he drew back another arrow. Eurymachus charged Odysseus when he realized his lies weren't working but was cut down before he took two steps.

Next Odysseus came across Amphinomus. "Sire! I showed you courtesy and hospitality when you arrived!"

"And I warned you to leave," Odysseus snarled back. "But you chose to return to your lecherous ways hoping to steal my throne!" It was last thing Amphinomus heard as Odysseus let loose anther arrow.

One by one, the suitors fell. By early afternoon, they were all dead. The banquet hall was a slaughterhouse with blood and carnage everywhere. At the front, Eumaeus and Philoetius held the twelve disloyal servants at sword point as Odysseus approached them.

"Eumaeus and Philoetius," he said, "have these twelve clean this banquet hall. It shall be spotless by tomorrow morning, or they will regret that their mothers ever gave birth to them." He looked at them and continued. "You two have been loyal and true servants to this house during my long absence. You have assisted me in regaining my throne. For this, you both will be awarded great estates and will be joining the ranks of noblemen."

"Thank you, sire," they said.

The next morning, the banquet hall was cleaned as ordered. It was time for Odysseus and Telemachus to issue the final punishment to the disloyal servants. Telemachus approached them and spoke. "One act alone will not erase the treachery and debauchery you have done to this family." Then he turned to Eumaeus and Philoetius. "Take these twelve out and hang them. Then have the banquet hall cleansed one more time so their stench is no longer present."

With the final punishment issued, Odysseus had one more thing to do. He entered the private apartment where his wife Penelope, her attendants, and Eurycleia had remained since the battle yesterday. He could not rush this because he knew it was a great shock to his wife. He had to have her accept him and not force it upon her. This would take time and patience, but there was one thing he could do. "Eurycleia, you have been a loyal and true servant. Your final years shall be in spent in comfort, and you shall want for nothing."

"Thank you, sire," Eurycleia replied.

Then he turned to his wife. "My Lady," he said with a bow.

Penelope was dumbfounded. Every emotion possible was running through her. *Could this be my husband*? she wondered. She always knew he would return, but this could just as easily be another deception to steal the throne. It could even be an Olympian trying to seduce her. She had to test him.

"My husband," she began. "It's been a long time. Our son Telemachus was only a toddler when you left."

She's testing me, Odysseus though. He was glad she was. His wife wasn't going to accept any man who just entered her life as her husband.

"Our son was only an infant when I left, My Lady," he replied.

"True, but you went willingly to war, for the glory and riches."

"I tried to prevent the war by taking a delegation to see King Priam of Troy to bargain for Helen's release, My Lady. I even tried to fake insanity to keep from leaving."

"True. Fifteen years can play tricks on one's mind."

"Twenty years, My Lady," he replied.

The questioning went on for hours with Penelope asking questions only her husband would know and Odysseus answering them correctly. Then she thought of a question that would prove for sure if this man before her was her husband.

"If you are truly my husband, then you should be able to tell me every aspect of our bed and how it was constructed. If you like, I can have it brought out here and you and point out every part of it to me."

Odysseus smiled. "My Lady, our bed chambers have been blessed by the Olympian Hera so no one can enter it except you and I. Not even the Olympians would dare look into our chambers after Hera's blessing." Then he looked straight at her. "I built our bed with my own hands, and you know as well as I that it cannot be moved because one of its legs is the trunk of a tree that is growing in our chambers."

Penelope was overcome with emotion. Only her husband would know that fact about their bed. She began to weep as she fell into his arms.

"Yes, my dear Penelope. It is I, Odysseus, and I have finally returned."

CHAPTER 18

Forgiveness

Athena stood on a hill watching Odysseus as he began his latest task. A lot had happened in the month since the suitors were slain, but this was by far the most important thing he needed to do.

First the families of the suitors wanted revenge. They wanted to slay Odysseus and Telemachus for killing their loved ones even though Odysseus tried to settle things through negotiations. They tried to assassinate them several times. Finally, both sides gathered their forces and were about to do battle when Athena suddenly appeared.

"How dare you take up arms against your king!" Athena told the families. "You let your family member dishonor your king and disgrace your good name by trying to steal his throne when you all knew he would return. The Fates had decreed he would, and you still let them invade his household and dishonor his Queen. Anyone who takes up arms against Odysseus, his family, or his house shall feel my wrath! In addition, you will restore his family fortune because your family members squandered it during his absence."

Terrified at the prospect of facing Athena's wrath, the families returned home, never to take up arms again, and they restored Odysseus's fortune. Then Odysseus pardoned the suitors families so that no one could ever punish them for their actions. Next, Odysseus took the Phaeacian treasure and gave it to the families of the six hundred men who left for Troy with him and never returned. They suffered just as much as his family, and they deserved something for their loss.

These actions endeared Odysseus to his people ensuring their loyalty and accepting him as a wise and just king. Now Odysseus was about to do the most important thing of all since his return.

For the past month, Poseidon had been occupied with his vendetta against the Phaeacians for helping Odysseus return to Ithaca. He went before Zeus claiming they shamed him before the other Olympians and that he would never earn their respect if he did not punish the Phaeacians. Zeus agreed even though the Phaeacians were only following the rules of hospitality, something Zeus championed. Athena thought this was strange but didn't question her father's wisdom. As punishment, Poseidon put a curse on the Phaeacians. Any ship entering their harbors would turn to stone and sink. Ships could leave but none could enter. For a seafaring nation like the Phaeacians, this would be a slow agonizing death. With his vengeance complete, Athena knew Poseidon would turn his attention back to Odysseus and finish what he started.

At the edge of the sea, Odysseus gathered a large number of gifts, but it wasn't the gifts that would make a difference. He took a knee and began to speak. "Oh, Great Poseidon, Olympian of the Seas, hear my plea. I know I have earned your vengeance for blinding your son and mocking your name. I, my family, and our kingdom have suffered greatly from your wrath. I humbly ask that you accept my apology, accept these gifts, and forgive me and those who helped me after what I have done."

Athena smiled. It was simple yet honest. Not a trick to have Poseidon forgive him, but a heartfelt apology for what he had done. As she watched, she heard footsteps behind her. It was her brother Hermes.

He put his arm around her shoulder. "You did well, Sister," he said. "You brought Odysseus home, took care of his wife, and raised his son while he was gone. No other Olympian would have done what you did. No matter what happens, you have done what you can for Odysseus and his family." Then he looked straight at her. "I'm proud to call you my sister."

A tear formed in Athena's eye. "Thank you, Brother," she said. With that, they left and returned to Mount Olympus.

Athena and Hermes weren't the only ones watching Odysseus that day. From atop another hill, Poseidon himself was watching what was happening. He was about to strike Odysseus down when he heard him speak. The words did something to the Poseidon that rarely happened to the Olympian—they moved him. He remembered that Odysseus was a man of the sea and was the one who brought down his hated enemy, the Trojans. Yes, he had maimed his son and insulted him, but Odysseus suffered terribly in the ten years since leaving Troy. Seeing his men devoured by Polyphemus then losing most of his men to the Laestrygonians, being tormented by Circe, having to face the Sirens, forced to choose between Charybdis and Scylla, watching Zeus kill the last of his crew, the loneliness on Calypso's Island, and the suitors trying to steal his kingdom was more pain than a hundred men would face in a lifetime. He realized Odysseus had suffered enough. Now it was time to end his vendetta.

"Yes, Odysseus," Poseidon said, "I forgive you and all those who helped you." With that, a bright sky appeared over all of Ithaca, and he removed the curse on the Phaeacians. Ships could once again enter their harbors.

As Poseidon stood there watching, he felt a hand on his shoulder. When he turned to look, he saw Zeus smiling as he stood beside him. "You did well, Brother," he said. "For the greatest gift anyone can have is the gift of forgiveness. Because you forgave Odysseus, I will grant you this: if your son Polyphemus can change his ways and become more civilized, I will restore his sight."

"I will see that he does," Poseidon said. "Thank you, Brother." This caused Poseidon to think about the mistakes he made in his life—his feud with Athena, his anger at the Phaeacians, his revolt against Zeus. That last thought suddenly made him realize something. He turned and looked at his brother.

Zeus smiled. "Yes, Brother," he said, "I forgive you too." And with that, they left and returned to Mount Olympus.

Finally, after twenty years, Odysseus's journey was over.

THE END

About the Author

G. W. Brunswick was born and raised in Middletown, Ohio and is a graduate of Ohio Northern University, Ada Ohio with a Bachelor of Science degree in Electrical Engineering. His passion for reading has allowed him to create Greek mythology and science fiction novels filled with excitement and drama. *The Odyssey: An Adventure for the Ages* is G.W.'s first Greek mythology novel. G.W. currently teaches Industrial Maintenance Technology at a community college in Western Kentucky. He enjoys passing on his technical knowledge and skills to the next generation of students.